CADEN'S LITTLE GIRL

PEPPER NORTH

Copyright © 2025 by Stormy Night Publications and Pepper North

All rights reserved. No part of this book may be reproduced or transmitted in any form or by any means, electronic or mechanical, including photocopying, recording, or by any information storage and retrieval system, without permission in writing from the publisher.

Published by Stormy Night Publications and Design, LLC.
www.StormyNightPublications.com

North, Pepper
Caden's Little Girl

Cover Design by AllyCat's Creations

This book is intended for *adults only*. Spanking and other sexual activities represented in this book are fantasies only, intended for adults.

CHAPTER 1

Brooklyn snuck another peek at the handsome military man next to her. She hadn't been comfortable around men for months. Ever since... She shook her head to erase the angry face that loomed in her thoughts. *No. I won't think of him.*

He'd driven her car away several blocks from the gathered newsies and onlookers who'd swarmed around her car after she helped Giana flee from her assailant before she pulled herself together enough to note her location. Brooklyn forced herself to break the silence that filled the interior of her car. "Thank you for your help. I was too shattered by the chase to navigate out of there. I don't want to put you out anymore. I bet you need to get back to the base. Is there a back entrance or somewhere convenient where I could drop you off?"

"Trying to get rid of me?" he asked, drawing his words out slowly with a Texas accent that poured over her like warm honey.

As Brooklyn pondered the implications of how a voice could be so damn sexy, she caught his sideways glance toward her and rushed to answer. "No. I just don't want to impose. You definitely weren't expecting to have me screech to a stop on base and need Prince Charming to come save me."

"Prince Charming, hmm? I think I like that."

She turned in the seat to stare at him in disbelief. Who was this guy? He was older—not like her father's age, but more seasoned than the other soldiers who had rushed to Giana's aid. He also didn't react like any man she'd ever met before. "Maybe I should call you Caden?"

"That works too," he agreed and smiled at her.

Holy moly. That smile is lethal. She squashed the arousal that flared inside her. *Men are bad. Dangerous.* Her mind argued with the self-preservation warning system she'd built up over her time with her ex.

"Are you okay?" he asked. "Should I pull over?"

"Yes. Stop anywhere," she agreed quickly.

To her amazement, he did. Caden steered into the first parking lot he came to and parked the car before twisting in his seat to meet her gaze directly. "Brooklyn, he's locked up for a while. Tom can't get you."

"That's good. Thanks again for helping me," she told him.

"Do you want me to get out?" he asked.

"Yes, please." Brooklyn was polite automatically as her mind raced several steps ahead to returning to the apartment and grabbing her stuff. She needed to be out of town before Brent saw her on the news.

"I won't hurt you."

That pulled her out of her plans. "Of course not. You're not that kind of guy."

"Then why are you so eager to get rid of me?"

"It's better for you to get far from me," she forced herself to explain. When that concerned expression she'd noted as he protected her from the press reappeared, she added, "I have a crappy ex who habitually beats up on me and anyone stupid enough to be anywhere around me. You do not strike me as dumb."

"I try to avoid that."

Brooklyn waited for him to say something else, but silence filled the car. She hadn't explained herself well. "I stick to myself because I don't want anyone else's pain on my conscience. I'll pay for an Uber to take you back to base. I've got to empty my apartment and find a safer place to stay."

"You're safe with me, Brooklyn."

She laughed hoarsely. "That's what my last boyfriend said too. He ended up in the hospital with a skull fracture. Seriously, Caden, get out of the car and forget we ever met."

To her surprise, Caden shifted the car into reverse and pulled out of the parking space. "What are you doing?"

"Give me a minute." He tugged his phone out of his pocket and selected something on the screen. Instantly, she heard a ringtone.

"Who are you…" She snapped her jaw shut when he held up a finger to signal her to be quiet.

"Caden? We're starting a ten-mile hike. Did you change your mind about taking the day off?" a deep voice asked.

"Not exactly, Jerico. Bring the team. We need to move Brooklyn now."

She shook her head vigorously, mouthing the word no.

"At Giana's old complex?" the other man answered. "Bring a van?"

"Yes. Time is essential," Caden stressed.

"We'll be there in fifteen minutes." The phone disconnected.

"What are you doing?" Brooklyn demanded.

"Playing Prince Charming."

* * *

NEVER IN HER life had anyone taken charge of everything like Caden did. Pissed off at first by his insistence in helping her, Brooklyn's emotions shifted almost instantly to gratitude and amazement. Now standing in her empty apartment, Brooklyn checked her watch. Twenty-two minutes. That's how long it had taken for the buff men to pack her things into her car. The van hadn't been necessary. She'd wanted to have her possessions in her vehicle in case she needed to leave quickly.

"What have we missed?" Caden asked, walking through the place, opening cabinets and doors.

"Nothing. I can't believe how fast you all gathered my things. Thank you."

"If you'd let us pack your clothes, we could have shaved five minutes off the time," he said with a smile.

She pressed her hands to her cheeks to cool them off as she blushed again. The flashback of seeing her cotton panties in a stranger's—Caden's—hands as he efficiently folded them into her suitcase still horrified her. Thank goodness she didn't wear scraps of lace butt floss like other fancier women did.

"Could we not talk about that?" she whispered.

"Of course, little girl. I'm sorry. I didn't mean to embarrass you."

He looked so concerned that she rushed to reassure him. "I'm being silly. Thank you for your help. I can't believe you brought your team here to help. Everyone was so nice."

The minute she finished thanking him, his words replayed in her brain. Little girl? That phrase sent a shiver of excitement through her. But he couldn't mean that like a daddy would say, right?

Caden stepped closer. Brooklyn's skin tingled as if he were magnetic. What was it about this guy that attracted her so viscerally? His powerful body and self-assurance lured her toward him. His attitude screamed, "I can protect you from harm." That wasn't real, of course. Brent had erased any illusion of safety from her world.

"Do you have somewhere to go?" Caden asked, running his hand lightly down her arm.

Brooklyn loved the light touches that he used. A warm hand on her back as he ushered her into a room. The brush of his arm against hers when he relieved her of a heavy box. This reassuring contact. *He can't be this wonderful.*

Taking a step away from him, Brooklyn missed his warmth immediately when his hand dropped to his side. "I'll go turn in my keys, and I can be off. Let me lock the door and then you can go back to training."

"You didn't answer my question," he reminded her as he walked into the hall with her.

"What question?" she asked, hoping he'd drop it.

"Go turn in the keys, and we'll figure it out."

"Oh, you don't have to wait for me." Brooklyn hustled toward the office, calling her thanks to the team who'd helped.

"Take care, Brooklyn," Jerico called.

She'd enjoyed meeting the guys. Caden had an amazing team. Jerico, who looked like a hot, ripped Boy Scout. Who was she kidding? They were all handsome as hell and built like they could wrestle a bear and win. Koa, with his island handsomeness and savage tribal tattoos. The team medic was tough as nails in a safeguarding way. The massive Max, who bulged with so many muscles Brooklyn bet he could bench press her car. He had stowed her belongings in her trunk with a precision she'd never understand. Brooklyn wished she had a phone to take a picture of the arrangement so she could attempt to recreate it. And Hank. Slightly distant, Hank had an air of sadness. She'd wondered about his backstory before pushing the mystery out of her head. Brooklyn wouldn't be around to figure it out.

Coming out of the office with the receipt for her payment to end the lease, Brooklyn studied the building she'd hidden inside for several months. Her apartment had provided a refuge for her to heal and regain her strength. It was time to move on now. Not only because of Tom and the skirmish with Giana; Brooklyn had a weird feeling that Brent was zeroing in on her location. She hadn't spotted his silver sports car since she'd moved here, but had studied a warning posted by the mailboxes of a fuzzy image of a man with brown hair. Something about the image triggered a warning inside her. Could it be Brent?

The truck the soldiers had driven had disappeared, signaling they'd left. A sigh eased from her nostrils. Brooklyn hadn't understood how alone she'd felt until she'd had people around again today. Hearing the men ribbing each other and working together to empty her apartment had provided companionship.

CHAPTER 2

Walking back to her car, Brooklyn replayed the interactions of the day. Fleeing with Giana, meeting the guys, and packing up her belongings hadn't been on her schedule for today. And she'd just lamented her boring life yesterday when she sat alone in her apartment for the umpteenth day in a row.

"Bitch! I knew I'd find you."

Brooklyn stopped in her tracks, and her blood turned to ice as she recognized that voice. She turned to dash back into the apartment office, but froze when he spoke again.

"If you run, I'll hurt them as well. As far as I can tell, one woman is alone in there. She'll be easy to hurt before I drag you away."

"Please send officers to the Williams Estate apartment complex, building B. A man is loudly threatening a female resident."

A broad body stepped between Brooklyn and Brent. A torrent of relief flooded Brooklyn as she recognized those muscular shoulders and the close-cropped hair. She couldn't let him get hurt. This was her mess.

"Caden, you need to leave. He's not stable," she hissed for the military man's ears only.

"Looks like we've got a hero here, Brooklyn. Want to tell him what happens to good guys who interfere?" Brent snarled.

"He's leaving, Brent. I'll go with you." Brooklyn stepped to the side to duck around Caden's powerful body.

"You're not." Caden's voice was hard and definite. "Yes, ma'am. He's escalating. Get someone here now." Caden wrapped an arm around behind him as he shifted in front of her again. "Take my phone and stay there, Brooklyn."

"If I go with him, he'll leave you alone," she whispered, automatically following Caden's instructions and grabbing his phone. "Don't get involved. He could do anything."

"Exactly," Caden told her.

Even from behind, she could tell Caden never took his eyes off Brent. The dispatcher's voice caught her attention, and Brooklyn pressed the phone to her ear. "I'm Brooklyn Montague. I have a restraining order against Brent Maldoney in the state of New York."

"What's happening now?" the policewoman asked.

"Brent has stalked me for over a year. I moved here to escape from him. He's threatened to hurt the woman in the apartment office if I don't go with him. An innocent bystander is blocking his access to me. Hurry! He's not…"

"Hang up the phone, bitch! The police can't stop me from making you pay," Brent bellowed.

"A squad car is ten minutes away. Keep him talking," the woman told her as Brent spoke to Caden.

"A soldier boy, huh? Brooklyn was always a diseased whore. Why don't you leave and get yourself checked out?"

A snicker came from the building next to her, and Brooklyn died inside. A few residents drawn by Brent's yelling had walked out on their balconies to watch and film the drama.

"We both know that's a lie," Caden answered calmly.

"Do we?" Brent taunted. "I don't hear you denying you've fucked her."

"Our relationship isn't your business," Caden assured him, sounding cool and collected.

Astonished, Brooklyn realized Caden was in complete control of his emotions. Nothing Brent said to him triggered Caden to react rashly. A familiar snick signaled Brent had flipped open his favorite hunting blade. Her already pounding heart lurched in her chest.

"Hurry! He's pulled out a knife," Brooklyn said into the device in her hand before warning Caden. "Be careful, Caden."

"Stay back, Brooklyn," Caden warned. His head never turned, and his gaze remained focused on the other man.

Hope jolted through her when the sound of a siren reached them. *Please let them hurry!*

Caden jumped backward, causing Brooklyn to scurry out of his way. A flash of a blade caught her eye, and she met Brent's evil gaze. Fear ran down her spine, tensing her muscles. His face contorted with rage, and pure hatred shone in his eyes. She stood frozen in place. Why did he hate her so much?

"There you are, bitch!" Brent lunged toward her.

A powerful arm wrapped around her waist, lifting Brooklyn off her feet. She shrieked and flailed her arms and legs, trying to get free from her captor.

"It's me, little girl," Caden said as he yanked her away from the slash of the gleaming hunting knife. "Run to the office."

She couldn't leave him. Caden was in danger because of her. She had to help him. As the blare of the siren strengthened, Brooklyn looked around for anything to throw at Brent. Reaching down, she grabbed a handful of the decorative stones in the landscaping.

"Drop the weapon. I don't want to hurt you," Caden warned in a low, emotionless tone that chilled her. In total control, Caden spoke like this was a normal day in his life.

Stepping to the side, Brooklyn heaved the rocks at Brent. Only a few pinged off their assailant as others tumbled to the ground. Time froze for an endless second before Brent extended his knife and ran toward her.

Caden moved so quickly, Brooklyn had trouble tracking the action. Brent tumbled to the ground with Caden following him. A flurry of curses burst from Brent. Caden silently stripped the blade from Brent's hand and pinned his arms behind his back, pressing their assailant's face to the dirt. The screech of brakes signaled the arrival of the police.

"Head over to the squad car, Brooklyn. Explain what's happening," Caden requested in that quiet, controlled Texas drawl.

This time, she followed his directions. "Officer, I have a restraining order against that man on the ground in New York. He came after us with a knife," Brooklyn said.

"I saw it all, Officer. That man attacked them," the manager called from the office. Several neighbors echoed her words. One even offered the videotape of the incident.

In a few minutes, Brent sat handcuffed in the back of the squad car. The out-of-control man's shouts reached her as she stared in horror at his frantic motions that rocked the vehicle.

The image of his enraged face would show up in her nightmares. Only then, no reinforced glass would separate them. Warm hands turned her from the view. "It's over, little girl. You're okay. He can't hurt you ever again."

"You haven't ever dealt with the justice system. He gets

away with everything repeatedly. I'll never be safe. He'll keep coming after me," she whispered and wrapped her arms around herself.

Caden pulled her close and held her tight. She melted against his powerful frame. He'd kept her safe.

"Thank you for helping me." A thought popped into her head, and she took a step backward. "Did he hurt you?" She ran her hands over his body, searching for an injury.

"I'm fine, Brookie. He didn't get anywhere close to me with that knife," Caden assured her.

She shuddered as her mind replayed Brent's lunge toward her. "I hit and kicked at you. Did *I* hurt you?"

"I might have a bruise on my shin and on my stomach tomorrow. You pack a wallop."

"Oh, no. Let me see!" Brooklyn yanked up Caden's T-shirt to check.

A loud roar sounded from the car. Caden tugged his shirt out of her hands and drew it back into place. "It's probably better if you wait to undress me until your ex is gone." Caden's blue eyes danced with amusement.

"Don't laugh. He's unbelievable. I'll get on the road and be out of town before they release him."

"How long have you been running, little girl?" he asked, sobering immediately.

"Too long. A year, eighteen months maybe. We broke up almost three years ago. I stayed in New York, sure that the system would protect me. I got a lawyer and a protective order. He put me in the hospital the following week. I'd pissed him off."

"He went to jail then, right?"

"Brent was out before I was. His parents bailed him out and then drove him to the hospital. My nurse heard me screaming and called security. That time, they kept him for two days. I convinced the doctor to release me the next day."

"And you took off?" Caden asked, his face dark with anger. He turned to watch the squad car drive out of the apartment complex. Brent's yelling face still focused on them through the back windshield.

"He found me a week later. Brent had placed an AirTag on my car. That started it. This time, I lost him for a few months. I'd started to think it was over. He'll never stop," Brooklyn told him, brushing a tear away that tumbled down her cheek. "Thank for packing my car. I'll be able to put some miles between us before they release him again. They never keep him for long."

"I don't like the thought of you out there alone, Brooklyn."

"Don't worry. I've survived this long. My folks send me money to exist on. I'll go to a hotel somewhere tonight and update them. They keep track of me and all the charges filed against him. Maybe someday, Brent will rack up enough crimes to get thrown in jail for a few years."

Brooklyn shook her head and walked over to her car. Caden paced alongside her. She loved it when he wrapped an arm around her. Standing close to him, she couldn't imagine Brent daring to attack her. If only…

"You have another option, little girl."

"I really don't, Caden."

"You could stay here with me. My team and I would protect you. Bullies like Brent usually choose another target when the one they're focused on isn't an easy victim."

"I don't want any of you to be targeted," she said quickly.

"Everyone needs help, little girl. Let me finish this for you."

"Why would you offer to get involved?" Brooklyn dug her hand into her pocket to pull out her keys as they reached her car.

"I've looked for someone special for many years. I think

you might be the one I've searched to find," Caden told her. He gently wrapped his hands around her shoulders and turned Brooklyn to face him.

"Me?" She glanced at him in surprise. He felt the connection between them like she did? "You could do much better than me. Even if I didn't have an out-of-his-mind stalker."

"Never talk badly about yourself, Brooklyn," he told her in such a stern tone that she shivered in reaction. "You should know that I'm a daddy."

His blunt words caught her off guard. "A daddy? Like of little…" Brooklyn's voice trailed away as she realized he'd called her a little girl several times. She hadn't remarked on it because she was younger than he was. She'd figured he considered himself like a father to her—not a 'daddy.'

"Yes, Brooklyn. A daddy. If I haven't read you wrong, you are a precious little girl."

"I'm twenty-three, Caden. Fully grown," she told him, not answering the implication in his words. She tore her gaze from his and focused on the keys in her hand.

"Brooklyn. Please look at me."

She shook her head. Could this day get any worse? A car chase, Brent finding her, now a guy who somehow guessed her secret fantasies.

"Brooklyn, have I shown you any sign that you can't trust me?"

"No," she whispered and peeked up at him.

"Thank you, sweetheart. I can't let you run. If you're right and they release Brent today, tomorrow, whenever, your chance to make this endless loop of harassment end will evaporate. Come home with me. I can protect you."

"He's dangerous."

"He hasn't met dangerous yet, little girl."

"You?"

"Yes. I can make sure you're safe. And we can explore this link between us," Caden suggested.

"I'm really tired of running. It sucks."

"Then let's stop it."

Before she could stop herself, Brooklyn stepped forward into his arms. He squeezed her tight and ran his hand over her hair. "This is the day everything changes for you, little girl. Thank you for being brave."

CHAPTER 3

"Let me get out to open the door and we'll stash your car in the garage," Caden urged when they arrived at his house. He'd already called his team to request that the guys drive his car over for him from the base. They'd agreed without asking questions.

Her body vibrated with nervous energy. Caden couldn't imagine her stress level after months of Brent's targeting. The military had equipped him with skills to handle the impact of enemy attacks. Caden could endure a lot, but he wasn't under a constant threat. And he had his team backing him up. Brooklyn was alone and vulnerable.

He kept his explanations calm and simple, trying to soothe her. He would need to reinforce that his intentions were supportive to reassure Brooklyn that she was safe with him. Guessing that her safety required always having an escape plan, he pointed to a glowing white box on the wall and told her, "The control for the automatic garage opener is there by the door into the house."

She nodded and whispered, "Thanks." Her rigid posture softened slightly.

After pulling slowly into the garage, Caden turned off the engine and popped open his door. She stepped out as well and studied his meticulously clean and organized garage.

"Wow. I think you could eat off the floor out here."

"Military training at its finest. Come inside. I'll show you the guest room, and you can decide what you'd like to bring in." The guys had packed her things in the trunk alone. She hadn't had much—a suitcase of clothes, a set of sheets, a few boxes, and some cleaning supplies.

"I guess we could have brought my food over instead of tossing the fruit and stuff," she told him, looking around as he led her into the house. "Good heavens. Dust doesn't stand a chance here, does it?"

Caden chuckled. "Thinking you've moved in with a clean freak?" he asked. "Don't worry. I don't expect anyone else to follow my routine. When I moved in, I set up different tasks for different days. Monday is mop day. On Tuesdays, I clean the bathrooms. And so on."

"I can help with that. And I'm a pretty good cook," she rushed to tell him.

"Little girls don't cook in my house, Brooklyn. Your room is down the hall here."

He stopped at a closed door and met her gaze. "Whatever you don't like, we can change, Brooklyn." He turned the doorknob and caught himself holding his breath. Would she like it?

Brooklyn stepped into the middle of the room and turned in a circle as she wrapped her arms around her chest. He watched her gaze rest on different items in the room: the adult-size crib, the changing table with the padded top, the rocker, the toy chest, and the colorful decorations. When she stopped, facing him, she whispered, "You *are* a daddy."

"I am. I put this room together a few months ago when I thought I'd found my little girl. She was a neighbor of one of my teammate's Little. We went out on three dates, but we both agreed almost immediately that she wasn't mine and I wasn't right for her."

"I'm sorry. You put this room together for her, and she left?"

"She never saw this room, Brooklyn," Caden told her. "I was confident I'd find the right little girl some time. Turns out she raced into my life without warning. Good thing I was ready for you."

"Are you sure you want me to stay in here? I could sleep on the couch."

"It would make me happy for you to enjoy this room. Shall we bring your things in here?" he suggested and saw her emotions flash across her face. Would she take a chance?

"Maybe my suitcase?"

"Let's grab it. I think there was a small case from your bathroom. Would you like that as well?"

"Oh, yeah. I have my body wash and my cosmetics in there. I haven't worn makeup for a while since no one saw me. I can spruce myself up."

"I haven't worn makeup for a while either," he teased. "I think you are perfect, just as you are. Let's see if we can find everything in your trunk."

She paused in the doorway to glance back at the bedroom one more time. When she turned with a big smile, Caden knew she loved the room. "Come on, little girl," he invited and held out his hand. To his delight, she linked her fingers with his and almost skipped next to him as they returned to the garage.

A few minutes later, Caden had pulled out her two cases. When he put a hand on the lid of the trunk to close it, she blurted, "There's one more thing I need."

"Of course. We can take everything inside if you'd like."

"Let me grab..." When Brooklyn leaned into the trunk,

Caden attempted not to focus on her gently rounded bottom and failed. His little girl attracted not only his protective side, but his desire as well.

Her derriere wiggled as she slid things around to grab a pillowcase wedged in the back. "Oh, no! It's stuck." Brooklyn stood, her face drawn with worry. "I can't get it out."

"Let's clear a path," Caden told her. He started pulling her things out of the trunk and stacking the small parcels to the side. "Good thing you had these boxes ready to pack."

"I keep them handy. It's hard to find one that I can carry," she explained.

Caden turned back toward the car to remove the next box and barely shook his head. No one should have to live planning to flee at a moment's notice. He fought down his anger at her ex, not wishing to scare Brooklyn. He vowed to make sure that this danger stopped now. One way or another.

As he moved the carton, the pillowcase popped free. A small, fuzzy paw emerged through the opening. Her stuffie. Caden grabbed the material and lifted it from the small space it had occupied. "Here you go, sweetheart."

"Thank you, Caden!" Brooklyn wrapped her arms around the bundle and hugged it close. To his absolute delight, she seemed to drift into Little space. Her body softened and relaxed as she twisted gently to rock her stuffie.

"Would you introduce me to your friend?"

Her cheeks turned rosy pink as her gaze focused on her ragged sneakers. She enchanted him as she stubbed her toe on the concrete while considering his request. "He's really shy."

"I promise I'll be nice and won't scare him. Could you vouch for me?"

Brooklyn studied him for a moment before ducking her head to whisper, "It's okay, Fluffikins. Caden kept me safe from You Know Who. I think we can trust him."

She reached inside and pulled out an adorable caramel-colored bunny with long floppy ears with a tattered pink ribbon around its neck. Caden guessed immediately that Brooklyn had loved this stuffie for many years. He smiled at the picture they created together as she hugged her bunny to her chest.

"Hi, Fluffikins. I'm very glad to meet you. I bet you'll love bouncing around the nursery."

"Caden's going to let us stay with him for a while. Isn't that nice of him?" Brooklyn said in a bubbly voice.

"You carry Fluffikins inside. I'll bring the boring stuff," Caden told her.

"I could help."

"You are very sweet, but a daddy would never let a little girl carry something heavy. You lead the way and show your stuffie around."

Brooklyn nodded eagerly and walked back into the house. She gave Fluffikins a tour of the open family room and kitchen area before heading down the hallway. "In here is our room. It's so pretty."

Her luggage was incredibly light. Caden guessed she had the bare minimum of clothing and possessions. He hadn't seen the contents of all the boxes in her trunk, but he suspected most were shelf-stable foods, household staples like toilet paper, and some cleaning supplies.

He set her bags inside the door. "Would you like help unpacking?" he asked.

"Oh, I can leave everything in there. I'll pull out what I need."

"Unpack, little girl. I plan to keep you."

She stared at him for several seconds. "You mean like forever?"

"I like the sound of that. Perhaps you've run for long enough. Maybe it's time to find a place to call home."

Brooklyn's eyes filled with tears. Quickly, they cascaded down her cheeks. Caden's heart lurched in his chest. He hadn't meant to upset her. Moving toward her, he wrapped his arms around her torso and pulled her close.

"Hey, sweetheart," he started, not sure what to say to comfort Brooklyn.

He hugged her tighter when she rested her cheek on his chest and leaned against him. Her sobs continued. Caden swept an arm under her legs and picked Brooklyn up. She wrapped her arms around his neck, holding on like she was afraid he would disappear or drop her. Neither of those things would happen.

Caden sat in the rocker he'd put together a few months ago and cradled Brooklyn on his lap. Her free hand grabbed a fistful of his T-shirt and held on for dear life. Slowly, he rocked her. "Oh, Brookie. You are so upset. What did I say?"

She hid her face on his chest and didn't answer. Caden pressed a kiss to the top of her head, holding the delectable little girl close. He considered what he had said to her just before the tears started. "Did hearing the word home upset you?"

Brooklyn nodded with her nose still pressed to his chest.

"Do you miss your parents?" he asked, trying to guess what had made her so sad.

She nodded again.

"Are you crying because you haven't seen them for a while?"

She shook her head.

As Caden considered what he should ask next, Brooklyn whispered, "I miss having a home."

"Their house or your own?" he asked. Had Brooklyn always lived with her parents?

"I had a really nice apartment. It was small, but I painted

the walls blue and hung up a few pictures I rescued from someone's garbage. It was mine."

"That sounds amazing, little girl. I bet you loved living there." Caden stroked her back. To his delight, as he reassured Brooklyn, her breathing settled as her sobs eased.

"It was my happy place."

"And then you met Brent?" he guessed.

"The worst day ever. I was so stupid," she told him.

"No talking badly about yourself. That's my first rule," Caden said firmly. "I bet he was charming, and you were too young to pick up on his negative traits."

She leaned back and stared at him in shock. "How did you know?"

"Everyone usually has a love interest that teaches them what's important and what to avoid. For me, that person was Susan. I thought she was perfect and almost didn't recognize myself by the time I figured out she had taken over my life in a bad way."

"What did she do?" Brooklyn asked, focused on his face.

"My friends tried to tell me, but I didn't listen. Then I returned unexpectedly after being deployed for a couple of months. I surprised her at work. When I showed up at her office, they'd never heard of Susan Zigler. The receptionist called HR to double check."

"She'd lied to you?"

"That wasn't the worst lie. I headed to our apartment, thinking I must have screwed up what she'd said. I let myself into the apartment and found her in bed with someone else."

"Oh, Caden! I'm sorry." Brooklyn's brown eyes clouded with tears again.

Quickly, he assured her. "That wasn't a bad thing, Brookie. I needed to know. It was gut-wrenching at first, but when I think back, I could pick out a lot of warning signs I'd missed."

"Was she your little girl?"

"No. That was one of the big red flags I let pass. She had shared she had fantasies of being little, but resisted any attempts I made to be her daddy." His stomach still twisted into a sick knot when he thought about how she'd manipulated him and played on his desires.

"So, she lied?"

Caden smiled faintly at the anger in her voice. She didn't like that someone had behaved so badly. "Very definitely. That's one thing I am rigid about now. Don't lie to me, little girl. I can handle everything else, but lying makes me shut down."

"I don't like lying either."

"Can you tell me what happened to your beautiful apartment?"

"Brent. I met him in a class at community college. He was handsome and attentive. I was thrilled that he pursued me. Brent wanted to spend a lot of time with me. Finally, I invited him to move in."

"Things changed after he got to your apartment?" Caden guessed.

"He wouldn't let me see my friends and made me switch to online courses, so I didn't have to leave the apartment. He even painted the walls this light gray color, saying it was the new *in* tone. Eventually the space I loved became my prison."

"Did you move out?"

"When I tried to leave the first time, he hit me," she whispered.

Clamping down at the burst of anger that consumed him, Caden forced himself to focus on Brooklyn. "Oh, Brookie. I'm so sorry, baby."

"I filed a police report and kicked him out. The charges were dropped for lack of evidence. A 'he said, she said' situation, the cops told me. I packed up my stuff while he was out and ran. I've been running ever since."

Caden didn't trust himself to say anything. He clenched his teeth and continued to rock her. Brooklyn relaxed against his chest. When he had regained control from his urge to pound Brent into pulp, he suggested, "Shall we paint your room blue?"

She pushed away from his chest to look at him. Caden could see the hope in her eyes. "You don't have to do that," she told him.

"I don't have to, but I'd really enjoy making your space comforting to you. Hopefully, you'll feel like this is home."

"What if he comes here?"

"I'll stop him from bothering you in the future. This ends now," Caden promised.

He wouldn't allow this to continue. Bullies like Brent usually backed down when faced with a target that fought back. Caden had already shown Brent that he had the skills to take him down. Caden would have no trouble making sure Brent didn't get back up.

"I don't want you to get in trouble with the law," she told him.

"You let me worry about that, Brookie."

"Brookie?" she whispered. "No one's ever called me that."

"It seems to fit you. Do you want me to stop?"

She shook her head immediately. "No, I like it. I enjoy being here with you, Caden."

He cupped the back of her head and drew her lips to his. Caden kissed her softly at first. When her lips moved eagerly under his, he deepened the kiss. Her mouth opened, inviting him inside. Her taste was addictive. His hunger for her grew with each exchange.

When his control stretched thin, Caden forced himself to lift his head. Her hungry expression made his already thickening cock jerk in his fatigues. She affected him on a caveman level. He wanted to strip Brooklyn naked and stake his claim on her gorgeous body.

When she blinked her eyes open in confusion, Caden stroked her soft cheek, regretting the roughness of his working hands. "Welcome home, little girl. I'm warning you now, I'm a possessive bastard, but I'll always listen to your needs and concerns."

"Thank you. And thank you for rescuing me from Brent. I'm so tired of running from him."

"How about if you focus on exploring our relationship instead? Could you see me as your daddy?"

"Yes, please."

CHAPTER 4

"Caden!" she squealed and threw her arms around his neck when the handsome man who held her stood and whirled in a circle celebrating her answer. She couldn't help but giggle at his enthusiasm.

I guess he liked my answer.

On the other hand, Fluffikins was highly annoyed and glared at her from the rocker where she'd left him. Her bunny was a wild man who loved zooming around her apartment. Her stuffie would scold her if he didn't get to have fun too.

When Caden slowed down, Brooklyn's head spun delightfully. "Do it again! Fluffikins missed out on the fun!"

"We can't have that." Caden leaned over to pick up the stuffed bunny and tuck it into her hands. "Let's go the opposite way. Ready?"

"Yessss!" she cheered as Caden twirled them one more time.

This time when he stopped, Fluffikins looked happy. Her tension and worry evaporated when he held her. She couldn't believe how this dynamic man had made a scary day suddenly the best she'd had in a very long time. Hope for a much rosier future kindled inside her.

"Thank you, Caden."

"You're welcome, Brooklyn. Now, I need to feed us. Do you want to play here or come chat with me as I round up something for us to eat?"

"I'll stay with you. Fluffikins wants to take a nap."

"I don't blame him." Caden set her feet on the carpet and released her when she had regained her balance.

Drawn by the special bed with a railing around it, Brooklyn walked across the room to tuck her stuffie under the covers with his pink nose sticking out so he could breathe. Brooklyn didn't feel rushed or embarrassed to have him see her taking care of her bunny. He understood. She'd never met anyone like him.

Turning around, she walked back to him. Caden stood patiently, his body as relaxed as those muscles would allow. When she got close, he reached out a hand to her with a smile. When she took it, he squeezed her fingers playfully.

"Come on, little girl. Tell me what you like to eat."

"I can eat anything. Well, anything but slimy avocados. They're gross."

"I see." He paused for a minute as if he were thinking. "You're in luck. I'm fresh out of avocados. I could make grilled cheese sandwiches and tomato soup?"

"No soup for me, but I'd love a sandwich," she answered and clapped a hand over her stomach when it growled loudly.

"Sounds like your tummy is starving. I'll get toasting. Sit here and talk to me." Caden pulled out a high stool at the island for her.

"I could help," she suggested, shifting awkwardly from one foot to another.

"You can set the table for us in a few minutes. Keep me company while I put together the sandwiches."

Brooklyn gave in and levered herself up on the seat he held. Caden pressed a kiss to the top of her head before circling around the island. That small gesture of affection warmed her heart. On her own for so long, she craved human contact.

No, not just anyone's touch. She treasured every tender gesture Caden lavished on her. How had she found a man who checked off all her wants and needs? Was he real or pretending like Brent had?

"Breathe, Brookie. You're safe here," Caden said quietly.

Brooklyn looked up to see him focused on her with a concerned expression. "Sorry. I must have spaced out."

"If you're worried about something, talk to me."

"I'm okay," she told him quickly.

"But I want you to be fabulous." Caden winked at her and turned to grab a few things from the refrigerator.

His statement repeated in her brain. For what seemed like months, Brooklyn had simply existed. Hunted, she'd hidden in a series of apartments and hotels, scared Brent might knock on her door at any moment. Caden suggested she should reach for more.

"I'd like to be fabulous," she whispered, watching him cut the bread.

He paused to meet her gaze and smiled. "Then we'll make that happen. Tell me how you discovered you were Little."

Her cheeks heated. Brooklyn resisted the urge to look away from him in embarrassment. She forced herself to be brave and answer. "I found a book. I read it five times, over and over."

"What was it about?"

"A little girl who found her daddy at a BDSM club. Of

course, she had to go through several who were total jerks. But he rescued her and claimed her as his own."

"What was her name?"

"Dorie. She was tall and plump. She didn't think anyone would ever consider her as a little girl," Brooklyn shared, eager to share her favorite storyline.

"Little girls come in different shapes and sizes. Was Dorie a young Little or was she more of a Middle?" he asked, turning to grab a pan from the drawer next to the stove.

"Little Little," Brooklyn answered automatically, before realizing how much of herself she'd revealed. She tensed with panic. What would he think of her?

Caden didn't react with shock or aversion. He simply flipped on the gas and set the pan on the burner to warm. Soon the sandwiches toasted slowly. A delicious scent filled the kitchen area.

"That smells so good!" she told him.

"Fingers crossed I don't burn them." Caden told her as he reached up to the top shelf of a cabinet.

Brooklyn couldn't avoid noticing how he moved. Caden was handsome from the front and the back. Distracted, it took her a minute to see the items he removed from their packages. It was a set of pink dishes with tiaras printed on them.

He brought them over to the sink and washed them. Brooklyn struggled to find something to say. She loved the cute pattern on them. Should she let him see how excited she was?

"A grilled cheese sandwich will taste so much better on a cute plate, don't you think?" he asked.

She nodded. "Did you buy those for the other woman?"

"No, Brookie. I bought these for my little girl. Just like the nursery, I knew I'd find you someday. I'm excited for you to use these. Will you try them for me?"

"I'd like that," she whispered.

"Good girl. Let me flip these over before they burn."

She stared at the adorable pattern and wiggled happily in her chair. She'd never owned any Little stuff. Caden rejoined her on his side of the island. He dried the cup and filled it with milk before snapping on the sippy cup lid.

When he set it in front of her, Brooklyn stared at it. What would it feel like to take a drink from the spout? Watching his face, she reached for it, ready to abandon the cute container if he laughed at her. Her fingers brushed the plastic.

"Oh, no!" Her gaze ricocheted to the cup as it tumbled over. Horror filled her. She was such a klutz.

Caden moved quickly and righted it. "It's okay. Look how well your scientific experiment to test it went. There are exactly three drops of milk on the counter." He wiped them up with a paper towel, erasing her mistake. "And they're gone. Try another experiment. Take a drink. Does it taste any different in that fancy sippy?"

Brooklyn lifted it to her lips and took a drink. Cold milk slid down her throat as she swallowed. "It's milk," she answered, shrugging.

"Perfect." He paused and smiled at her. "I'm so glad I found you, Brookie. Oh, no! The sandwiches!"

Of course, the food was fine. Brooklyn didn't believe Caden could mess anything up. He handled everything with ease. She tilted her head, fascinated by him. Even when doing something as simple as slicing up an apple and cutting a sandwich into triangles without the yucky crust, Caden oozed control. Was there anything he couldn't do well?

"Oh! I'll set the table!" Brooklyn slid off the stool and carefully carried her cup to the round wooden table.

Caden met her there with napkins and forks. "Thank you, little girl. Let's have you sit here next to Daddy's chair."

"Daddy," she repeated in a whisper, peeking up at him.

"When you're ready, I'd love for you to call me Daddy." He lifted her chin and kissed her lightly before repeating, "When you're ready. Now, sit down and see if you approve of my grilled cheese."

"I'm sure it's wonderful," she told him, sliding into the chair he pulled out for her.

After putting her napkin on her lap to show him she had manners, Brooklyn took a bite of the sandwich. A long string of cheese stretched as she pulled the yummy treat away. She twirled it around her finger and popped it into her mouth when she'd finished chewing. "Absolutely incredible."

"I'm glad you like it," Caden told her.

Brooklyn couldn't believe how easy it was to talk to him. He didn't probe into her past, but told funny stories about his team. She could tell how bonded they were. Each seemed to know each other's strengths and weaknesses. Caden's perceptions of the other soldiers impressed her. His role as the team chief relied on his experience and insight into those he led.

"Did you always want to be a soldier?"

"Always. My father and grandfather were in the military. I guess it's in my blood."

"Isn't your job dangerous?" she asked, trying to look cheerful, while inside she worried.

"I won't lie to you, Brookie. My team deals with some unpleasant characters. That's why we train so hard. So we can get in, do the job we're given, and all return safely. We should talk about deployments."

Her appetite vanished. Brooklyn gripped her hands together under the table and asked, "You won't leave soon, will you?"

"My position deals with a lot of emergencies, sweetheart.

When my phone rings, I go. Let me grab a piece of paper and we'll figure out what you should do if you're here alone."

"Oh, I'll just leave," she blurted. He wouldn't want her to stay if he weren't here.

"You will not. This is your home now." His tone was stern and commanding.

She definitely didn't want to argue with him, but when he was gone, she would have to do whatever she needed to be safe. "I appreciate you want me to stay."

An 'eep' of surprise escaped from her lips as he plucked her out of her chair to sit on his lap. Automatically, she tried to slide off, but he held her firmly in place. "Caden…"

"Eyes on mine, little girl."

Slowly, she lifted her gaze to meet his blue eyes. His expression struck her—caring and concerned. "I will take every precaution to keep you safe, even if I'm not here. Your days of running are over, little girl."

"I hate looking over my shoulder. And…" She hesitated.

"And what, Brookie?"

"I don't want to go anywhere. I want to stay with you."

"And I want you here. So we make plans, and you stick around," he told her firmly.

"Okay. I won't run."

"Good girl. Now, I don't indulge very much, but I think this calls for a celebration. What do you think about fudge bars?"

"I love them."

Caden placed Brooklyn back on her chair and stood to grab their empty plates. "Let Daddy clean up and then we'll have our treat."

"Can I help?"

"Daddy's job. How about if you color me a picture for the refrigerator? That metal surface is so boring and sad."

"Do you have colored pencils?" she asked eagerly.

"Go check in that drawer there." He pointed to the bottom drawer of the desk at the side of the kitchen. "Anything in there is for you to play with. Leave the other drawers alone."

"Yes, Daddy." Brooklyn smacked her hand over her mouth. She hadn't meant to call him that. It slipped out.

"Repeat that for me, Brookie," he demanded, dropping the plates onto the counter with a clatter before walking back to her side.

"Yes, Daddy," she whispered.

"That makes me extremely happy, Brookie."

He whisked her back into his arms and twirled around in a circle, taking her breath away. She clung to him and laughed for the first time in many months. Her heart thumped inside her chest. She'd found someone who made everything better. "No," she corrected her thoughts. "I found my daddy."

CHAPTER 5

Dragging himself from the house had taken all his years of discipline. Caden was amazed how easily Brooklyn had settled in. The sight of her nestled in her crib with Fluffikins this morning had made him consider retirement for the first time. The military had always been his life. Funny how quickly she'd turned that around.

Before he'd sent her to bed, they'd worked on a plan for her to follow when he was deployed or simply out of the house. Most of the action steps required her to have a phone. He'd take care of that this afternoon on his way home.

"Guess we'll have a light day."

Caden looked up to see his team in a semicircle around him with expressions ranging from amusement to quickly concealed longing. Pulling his thoughts into the present, Caden zeroed in on Koa who'd made that suggestion.

"Thanks for inspiring our practice today, Koa. We're going to focus on medical evacuations. Team, you're down one member. The enemy blew up Koa's backpack of equipment. Unfortunately, a piece of the radio struck our communications operator in the head, leaving him with a dangerous head injury and questionable sanity. We need to get to the barracks on Chestnut in under sixty minutes to rendezvous with the helicopter. We're in the middle of enemy territory. Time starts now."

"Fuck!" Koa said, dropping the backpack and hitting the ground. "I hate being the dummy."

Max ran forward and scooped Koa over his shoulder as the group broke into a run toward the opposite side of the base. They moved into the shadows of the buildings to the tree line. Each member of the team contributed to their progress. They rotated who carried Koa to avoid overtaxing any individual. Caden worked with the team while noting places where they could make improvements. At sixty-seven minutes, they arrived at their target.

Caden announced the time. "We missed the transport. What could we have done better?"

Automatically, the men headed back to their starting point. They discussed where they lost unnecessary moments, potentially shaving off seconds here and there. The next time, they arrived three minutes late. On the third run through, the team had time to survey their surroundings and emerge safely into the clearing to dive into their imaginary helicopter.

"What do we take with us from this?" Caden asked.

"We don't let Koa have any more ice cream cones at our gatherings," Hank suggested, rubbing his shoulder.

"Hey! Thank your lucky stars you were carrying me and not Max," Koa protested, gesturing at the largest man on the team.

"Should we run it one more time with Max as our injury?" Caden asked.

"Nah. The weight wasn't the problem. It was the temptation to drop Koa on his head that slowed us down," Jerico said.

Everyone turned to stare at him in shock. Jerico was the last person anyone would have expected that ribbing to come from. Caden laughed, breaking the ice, and the others quickly joined him. Jerico was the newest member of the team, having joined them a few months ago. That joking comment showed Caden the group had truly bonded together.

Caden studied the group with a half-smile. The link between them would go a long way in keeping the men alive. He couldn't have planned this better.

* * *

KEEPING his focus on the training exercises had challenged Caden's discipline today. Rigidly, he'd kept his head in the game despite wishing he was back at home with his little girl. Caden had always planned on taking things slow when courting someone. Like his teammates, Caden had recognized Brooklyn as his own immediately, like a lightning bolt zinging through him.

By the end of the day, his ability to make small talk had evaporated. Caden focused on getting back to Brooklyn. He forced himself to stop and pick up the phone he'd reserved earlier in the day. A cute case with bunnies on it caught his eye at the store and went into the sack as well. She'd need some kind of protection for the device, right?

The house appeared quiet when he pulled into his driveway. His heart sank in his chest. She couldn't have left. Pounding up the two steps to his front door, Caden burst inside. He spotted a flash of pink and knew he'd scared her. Instant regret flashed through him. He shouldn't have imagined the worst. Why the hell hadn't he checked for her car in the garage? He tossed the phone on the couch, disgusted with himself.

"Brookie. It's me, sweetheart. I'm sorry I scared you," he called as he walked into the hallway.

When she didn't answer, he continued, "The house looked abandoned. I panicked, thinking you had left."

"You told me not to go." Her whisper came from under the crib. The bedding naturally draped over the edge of the bed.

"That's a great hiding spot, sweetheart. You thought quickly on your feet."

"Was this a test?" she asked. Caden could hear the outrage in her voice and knew he needed to tread carefully.

"No, Brookie. It wasn't a test. This was your daddy's fear exploding. I should have trusted that you'd stay true to your promise."

"That's right. You should have trusted me."

"Would you come out here so I can apologize?" Caden asked, needing to see her. He settled cross-legged on the floor next to the crib.

Seconds clicked by in the silent room. Finally, the bedspread twitched as a hand pulled it to the side. Brooklyn peeked out. Her eyes widened upon seeing him so close to her. Immediately, she scooted out.

Caden scooped her up in his arms and set her on his lap. He kissed her softly before saying, "Hi, sweetheart. I'm sorry I scared you."

"I wasn't sure what time you'd be home. Then someone banged on the door as they tried to get inside."

"I bet you thought it was Brent. That was frightening. How about if I come in through the garage from now on? I'll always be here around five. Today, I'm a bit late because I had to stop for something."

"What?" popped out of her mouth before she quickly said, "Sorry. That's not my business."

"You can ask me anything, Brookie. I may not be able to

answer if it's about work or the team, but I'll share what I can. How about if I show you what I picked up in a few minutes? I need to hold you now."

"Okay," she whispered.

Caden squeezed her tight and couldn't resist kissing her again. She had such a sweet nature. "I missed you today. Did you miss me?"

She leaned on his chest and nodded. "Fluffikins missed you a lot too."

"He'll be excited to learn that I ordered a food delivery with some special treats for him."

"Fluffikins doesn't like carrots," she told him, obviously guessing what he had purchased.

"A bunny that doesn't eat carrots? No way. I guess we'll have to eat them for him."

She shook her head vigorously. "Not me."

"That means more yummy carrot muffins for me."

"Carrot muffins? Are those good?" she asked, giving him the side-eye.

"Oh, yeah. Perhaps you'd try a taste for me? Just to see if Fluffikins might like them," he suggested.

"Maybe."

Caden knew that was the best he would get. "Thank you, sweetheart. Did you find the note I left you about breakfast and lunch?"

She hesitated slightly before answering. "Yes. I'm sorry I was such a lazybones this morning. I should have gotten up when you did."

"No way. My day starts way too early. Did you sleep well?"

"I don't think I moved last night. That... That bed is very comfortable."

He loved the pink tinge on her cheeks as she bumbled

with what to call the crib. "I'm so glad. Was the bed in your furnished apartment bad?"

"No. It was okay. This one seems so secure. I wasn't scared at all last night."

"It's been a long time since you felt safe, hasn't it?" he asked.

"I try not to think about that," she told him.

"Let's go see what I stopped to pick up." Caden boosted her to her feet and rose to take her hand.

Guiding her down the hallway, he pointed to the sack on the couch. "There it is!"

She rushed ahead to sit on the couch. "Can I open it?"

"Of course."

She pulled out the phone and looked up at him. "I haven't had a phone for a while. I ran over my old one when I figured out that he was tracking me with it."

"Good job, Brookie. I'm glad you thought of that. We'll be sure he doesn't get your phone number on this one."

"It was a scary time. I even went to a free clinic to make sure he hadn't given me anything. Like a disease. Trusting Brent didn't seem like a good idea."

When her face turned red, Caden guessed she hadn't planned to share that type of intimate information with him. "I'm glad you took care of yourself, Brooklyn. Zale tests the team routinely too. You're safe with me."

Her flushed cheeks turned a deeper red. To distract her, Caden pointed to the sack and said, "There's something else in there."

Eagerly, she thrust her hand back inside and pulled out the special case he'd found for her. "Bunnies! This is so cute!"

"The bunnies insisted on coming home with me. We'll get your phone set up after dinner." He glanced around the house and didn't see any signs that she'd been home throughout the day. "What did you do today?"

"I played in my room most of the day. Fluffikins wanted to explore all the fun stuff in there."

"I'm glad you enjoyed your room. What did you find for breakfast and lunch?"

"I... I wasn't hungry."

Her expression alone told him she wasn't telling the truth. "What did my note say?"

"Good morning and a bunch of stuff about breakfast and lunch," she answered.

"Hmmm. Did you have any trouble with the coffeemaker?"

"Oh, no. It was easy to figure out."

"Little girl. I think we've talked about lying," he said.

Her eyes widened. "I'm not lying."

"Brookie, my note apologized for my not having coffee in the house. It also suggested things you could eat. Tell me the truth. Did you ever leave your room today?"

"I went to the bathroom."

"You haven't eaten all day?"

"I wasn't hungry," Brooklyn told him. Unfortunately, her stomach chose that moment to growl loudly.

"You're certainly hungry now. Let me feed you, and then we'll deal with your untruthfulness." He stood and held out his hand to her.

She let him pull her to her feet, saying, "I'm sorry. I didn't want to invade your house."

"This is now your home, too, little girl. You're never an intruder here."

Caden helped her onto a stool at the island and reached into the refrigerator for an apple. Fingers crossed, she'd eat that. Quickly, he cut it into wedges and trimmed out the core, and handed her a slice.

"Start with this and I'll doll these others up a bit." He

spread peanut butter on the others and put them in front of her.

"Mmm, these are good," she mumbled around the treat as she devoured one coated wedge.

"Don't talk with your mouth full, sweetheart. I don't want you to choke. Just give me a thumbs up if you're chewing." He laughed when she answered with two enthusiastic thumbs up.

When she'd finished all the apple wedges, Caden held out a hand to help her off the stool. He drew her to the stuffed ottoman and sat down in front of her, steering Brooklyn to stand between his legs. "Now that you have something in your tummy, we need to deal with the lie you told Daddy."

"I'm sorry. I'll never do it again," she promised.

"You will. Little girls make poor choices sometimes. When you do, I will punish you. Tonight, I'm going to give you twenty swats to help you remember to tell Daddy the truth. The next spanking will be more severe. Do you have any questions, Brooklyn?"

"Is it going to hurt?" she asked, squeezing her thighs together.

Suspecting that was arousal mingled with apprehension, Caden didn't sugarcoat it for her. "Yes, little girl." He reached for her waistband and pulled her leggings down to her ankles. Guiding Brooklyn over his thighs, he was proud of her for not struggling or protesting. When he had her in position, he hooked a finger into her panties and exposed her bottom completely.

"No!" she yelped and struggled to slide off his lap.

Holding her securely in place, Caden reassured her, "Little girls get spanked on their bare skin, Brooklyn. Since this is your first time over my knee, I won't make you stand in the corner with your punished bottom on display afterward."

"I'm really sorry I lied," she whispered.

"This will erase the lie, Brooklyn, and you can have a fresh start." He lifted his hand and delivered the first smack. Brooklyn gasped at the sting. He admired the view as her pale skin turned pink.

Caden didn't draw out her discipline. He scattered the swats over her buttocks and upper thighs in quick succession. She tried to avoid his hand as quick gasps and protests fell from her lips for the first dozen slaps. Her movements revealed her shiny juices coating the tops of her thighs and confirmed his suspicion of her arousal.

"Daddy's got you, little girl. I'm so proud of you being brave," he praised her and watched her relax over his lap for the final few swats. "Good girl."

When he finished, Caden ran his hand over her red skin. "What a pretty spanked bottom. Everything is better now. No lies separate us. You deserve a reward, don't you?"

Brooklyn nodded without asking any questions. Draped over his lap, she tensed when he pulled her leggings and panties all the way off. "Spread your legs, Brookie."

After a pause, she shifted slightly. "More, little girl," he instructed and watched as she moved her thighs several inches apart.

"Good girl."

Caden trailed his fingers over her red bottom to her wet pussy. A gasp escaped from his little girl as he stroked her intimately. His cock, already steel-hard in his fatigues, jerked against the material. Her juices coated his fingers as he caressed her. Concentrating on those sensitive places that made her tense and inhale sharply, Caden focused on pleasuring her. Her body wiggled enticingly and she lifted her hips to press against his fingers as he tapped on her clit.

Damn, I'm a lucky man.

Her body tensed under his forearm braced on Brooklyn's

lower back to secure her in place. Caden thrust his fingers into her warmth and rotated his hand to continue to brush over that small bundle of nerves with his thumb. "Come, baby girl. Come all over my fingers."

"Daddy!" she cried out as her body shook with the force of her orgasm.

Gentling his fingers, Caden extended her pleasure with a light touch. When her body slumped limply over his lap, he gathered her into his arms and lifted Brooklyn to sit on his lap. He rocked her gently as he praised her.

"That's my very good little girl. Daddy is so proud of you."

"My lie is gone now?" she asked, searching his face.

"What lie?" he asked and kissed her forehead.

She nodded and leaned against his chest. "Thank you, Daddy."

"Shall we go have dinner now? I bet you're still hungry."

"Please, Daddy."

He redressed his little girl and took her hand to lead her back to her stool. Caden didn't allow himself to react when she hissed at the sensation of the hard wood on her punished bottom. That discomfort would remind her not to lie again.

CHAPTER 6

Their dinner, Caden repeated to himself as he opened his freezer, checking for something quick to fix. Thankfully, he enjoyed cooking and made large batches of dishes to freeze for nights he got home late or from missions and his fridge was empty. He grabbed a container of a cheat meal and popped it in the microwave to heat.

To stay in top physical condition, Caden watched what he ate and paid attention to nutrition. His twenties were long past. He couldn't fuel his body with junk and expect the level of energy and strength he needed to survive on missions. Considering Brooklyn's slim build and the fact she'd skipped breakfast and lunch, he suspected she was not as healthy as she should be. He definitely wasn't a purist with only healthy food in his house. There had to be a balance.

"What do you usually eat?" he asked.

"I'm flexible. I like peanut butter. It's super yummy on apples." She stopped and sniffed. "Is that lasagna?"

"It is. Do you like Italian food?"

"I am a mozzarella fanatic. Lasagna rocks!"

"What else do you like?"

"Oh, I'll eat anything."

"Except carrots?" he reminded her.

"Oh, I'm not big on vegetables. Or fish. It's too… fishy."

Caden chuckled. "I'll take you to my favorite fishing hole. There's nothing like fresh fried catfish."

Brooklyn wrinkled her nose, obviously not convinced. The beeping of the microwave interrupted their conversation. Caden poked at the lasagna and set it for ten more minutes.

"I'll set the table," Brooklyn volunteered.

"Thank you, little girl. The silverware is in that drawer, and the napkins are on the table."

He poured milk into a glass for him and a sippy cup for Brooklyn as she completed her task in silence. Her expression was focused as she folded the napkins and arranged the forks on the correct side. He mentally noted the importance of including her in activities. She wanted to contribute.

When the microwave beeped for a second time, he dished up healthy sized portions for them both and carried them over to the table. Normally, he'd eat a salad with such a heavy meal, but this lasagna was his own creation. He'd tweaked the recipe to include zucchini noodles and the traditional ones and layered in veggies as well. He hadn't anticipated serving it to his little girl, but it would provide a lot of nutrients he suspected she rarely got.

"You drink a lot of milk," she commented, taking a big drink from her cup.

"It's good for me and you."

"It would be better with chocolate added to it," she suggested.

"That would be fun for a change," he agreed, thanking Jerico's suggestion that he include it in his order. Koa, Jerico, and Zale had collaborated on what he should add.

Hank had come up with an idea that had made everyone stop and stare at him before each daddy pulled out their phone to make a note. Caden had added those to his list as well.

Brooklyn took a small bite and chewed happily. "This is so good." Her next bite was larger.

"I'm glad you like it," Caden said, eating a forkful as she poked at the stacked dish. He kept his amusement from showing on his face as she discovered his additions to the traditional dish.

"What's green in lasagna?" she asked.

"That recipe has zucchini and green peppers. It goes so well with the tomato sauce and cheese." Caden wouldn't try to fool her. That would only make her more hesitant to try things.

"I haven't ever had those in this dish before."

"What do you think?" he asked casually.

She took another bite and chewed. "Mmm. It's good. I usually only like zucchini raw with ranch dressing as a dip, but smothered in cheese is tasty."

"Awesome. I'm glad you like it." Caden changed the subject to avoid a discussion of anything else she hadn't discovered yet. "I don't suppose you made me another picture for the refrigerator?"

"I thought about it," she confessed.

"But the coloring books were in here," he finished for her.

"Yes." Brooklyn focused on her plate with a guarded look as if she were waiting for him to yell at her.

"Well, they'll be there tomorrow while I'm at work. Would you color one for me if you have time in your play schedule?"

Her eyes flew up to meet his. The corners of her mouth curled upward as she figured out he wasn't angry at her. "I'd love to."

"Perfect. Tonight, I thought we'd deal with the food delivery after dinner and maybe watch a cartoon."

"That sounds like fun. Isn't there something you'd rather see, like the news or something?"

"I listened to the news on the way home. Are you interested in what's going on in politics?" he asked.

Immediately, she shook her head. "No way. They just yell at each other and get angry."

"Unfortunately, they do that a lot. We'll stick to cartoons. Would you like Daddy to give you a bubble bath tonight?"

"Give me one?" she asked.

"Littles sometimes forget the bath part while they're playing in the bubbles. I have some fun tub toys."

"Oh." She took three more bites of her lasagna before peeking up at him again. "I've never had a daddy before, but usually in books I've read…" Her voice trailed off as if she struggled to say something.

"Brookie, you can ask your daddy anything you wish."

"You won't laugh at me?"

"Only if you tell me a knock, knock joke," he promised.

Caden noticed she'd stopped eating. He cut a piece of his lasagna and held it to her lips. Automatically, she opened her mouth for him to feed her. As she chewed, he tried to reassure Brooklyn.

"How about if I tell you the type of relationship I would like to have with my little girl? Then you can tell me if that matches what you're interested in or not."

She nodded eagerly.

"For me, being a daddy is both a nurturing emotional relationship and a physical one. I'm attracted to your little side as well as your beautiful adult body."

Seeing her cheeks blush an adorable pink, he offered her another bite as he continued, "When I met you, I wanted to wrap you in cotton and whisk you away from any threat. As I spend time with you, kiss you, and hold you, I get the impression that maybe you're attracted to me too."

Brooklyn looked down at her plate and then back up at him. She nodded.

"You're being so brave, little girl. I'm proud of you."

Caden took a bite himself, giving her a chance to think. When she finished chewing, he held her sippy cup up to her lips. Obediently, she took a drink. "Good girl."

The doorbell rang, and Brooklyn jumped to her feet. Caden wrapped an arm around her waist and pulled her close. "You're okay, sweetheart. That's the delivery guy telling me everything is here. Come sit on Daddy's lap and we'll grab the bags in a few minutes."

She eagerly climbed onto his thighs and leaned back against his chest. A warm sensation of rightness grew inside Caden's chest. He loved holding her. He pressed a kiss to her temple and stilled as Brooklyn turned her face to offer him her lips. Caden gave her several butterfly-light kisses until she leaned into the exchange, silently requesting more. He was happy to indulge her.

Deepening his kisses, Caden's desire for the precious woman escaped his ironclad control. His tongue swept into her mouth, tasting the deliciousness that lingered from their dinner as well as her own tantalizing flavor. He groaned into her mouth when Brooklyn threaded her fingers through his military-short hair. Returning the favor, he tangled one hand in her silky brown tresses and tugged her head back slightly.

Her answering moan signaled to him she enjoyed his domination and perhaps a hint of pain. His cock hardened at the image of spanking Brooklyn's bare bottom as she wiggled over his thighs. His fingers tightened in her hair, and to his delight she whispered, "Daddy, please."

Lifting his head to make sure she wanted more, Caden

loved the hungry expression on her face. "Are you okay, Brookie?"

"More kisses, please."

Caden lowered his mouth to hers and allowed himself to kiss her with all the emotions and desire inside him. To his delight, she matched his longing, revealing her need for him. Before he lost total control, Caden forced himself to end the exchange.

"Daddy!" she protested.

"I know, sweetheart. Daddy plans to make love to you very soon. I feel our connection deeply too, but I don't want to rush you. Once I make you mine, I'll never let you go."

She stared into his eyes for several long seconds before nodding. "I come with a lot of complications."

"I can't wait to discover everything about you. And sharing all I am," he assured her.

"I'd love that, too." Brooklyn hugged him tight. Caden rubbed her back, loving how well they fit together. He couldn't imagine a more perfect little girl. She was his.

When she leaned back, he glanced at his empty plate. "Someone stole my dinner. How about if we work on this plate now?"

He alternated feeding the adorable Little in his arms and himself until they couldn't eat another bite. "I think you like your daddy's cooking."

"Even if he sneaks vegetables in under the cheese," she said with an impish wink.

"Sounds like a perfectly Daddy thing to do." Caden swept her up in his arms and stood. He nibbled at that sensitive curve where her neck and shoulder met before setting Brooklyn on her feet. "Alright, my temptress, want to help me bring in the delivery?"

"Yes!"

When she rushed to the door, Caden called, "Let me open

the door, little girl." He checked the area outside before waving and picking up a couple of light bags for her to carry. "Put these on the island and we'll unpack everything."

"What are these, Daddy? They rattle!" She set them in the kitchen and pulled the first thing out. Looking at it skeptically, she said, "I think you got someone else's order."

"What is it?" Caden asked, following her with the other ten bags after locking the door behind him.

"There's several baby bottles and wipes—you know, like for baby bottoms," she reported, waving one bottle toward him to show him.

"Nope. This is my order. Do you like the cute animals on them?"

After checking out the pattern, Brooklyn whipped her head back up to stare at him. Her surprised expression enchanted him. "Did you get these for me?"

"I did. You enjoyed the sippy cups. I thought a bottle would be good for you before bed."

Her gaze dropped back to the bottle and then over to the wipes in her other hand. "And these?" she whispered.

Caden set down the other packages on the island and tugged her into the circle of his arms. "How much do you understand about your little side?"

She shook her head slightly as if the question was too complex to process.

"It's okay, Brookie. How about if we experiment and see what you enjoy the most?"

"You want me to wear diapers?" she asked, looking at him as if she expected to be pranked.

"Try them and see if your Little enjoys them. If you don't, then we know they're not for you."

"Are they for you? I mean... Is this something you'd like your Little to use?" She focused with laser precision on his face, trying to read his expression.

"You are the most important component in this equation. I want to take care of you to the extent *you* need."

"You're not answering my question," she pointed out.

"Sorry, sweetheart. I'll be direct for you. I have always been drawn to very little girls. Even though it might be scary or embarrassing in the beginning, I'm asking you to be brave. If diapers aren't for you, I'll get rid of them and we'll never talk about this in the future if it's a hard no for you."

"Can I think about it?"

"Of course. I think that's a great idea. Shall we see what else is in here?" he suggested, changing the subject.

"Are those Popsicle makers?" she asked, pointing to plastic forms poking out of a bag.

"Yes. Hank, one of my teammates, suggested them."

She froze and glanced up at him with a panicked expression. Caden could have kicked himself for spooking her.

"Do they know about these other things you ordered?" she asked, waving a hand over the items on the island.

"The food and drink items, yes. When I asked what juice they thought most people liked, Hank chimed in that he used to have these great Popsicle makers. He said grape and orange juices made the best frozen treats."

"Oh," she whispered as her fright lessened.

"I ordered some in case you might like to try them. What juice do you like best?"

"Grape first and orange is in second place."

"Then I'm glad I ordered both juices. See what's in that one," he suggested, nodding at the next sack.

Watching her face became his favorite activity. Her expression shifted between excitement and revulsion. Broccoli, bad. Pizza rolls, good. Caden was satisfied that he'd blindly chosen a few things she was excited to have in the house.

When the items sat on the counter waiting to be put

away, Caden suggested, "Let me turn on a cartoon for you while I find places for these goodies. I haven't seen Fluffikins for a while. What does he like?"

Her mouth rounded in a perfect O as Brooklyn remembered her stuffie. "I'll go get him."

In a short while, she'd curled up on the couch with her bunny in her arms. After a short debate, she settled on an old cartoon series Caden remembered loving as a kid. From the rapt expression on her face, Brooklyn enjoyed it tremendously.

CHAPTER 7

The sound of running water reached Brooklyn's ears. She was simultaneously nervous and excited. Baths meant no clothes. Would Caden see her naked or could she hide in the bubbles? Did he want to see her naked?

Brooklyn remembered the sensation of pressing tightly to his powerful frame as they'd kissed earlier. She hadn't reached down to touch him, but she was pretty sure his cock had hardened against her. Squeezing her thighs together, she imagined what making love with Caden would be like. He wasn't a teenager, but an experienced man. Of course, he'd had other partners. Maybe she wouldn't be as beautiful as they were. Or as good in bed.

The TV clicked off, making Brooklyn sit up quickly. She squeezed Fluffikins to her chest. *Please don't let me disappoint him.*

"I don't like that look, little girl. Are you scared?" Caden sat next to her and lifted her onto his lap. "Tell me what's going on in your brain."

"What if you don't like me?"

"I already like you, Brookie," he answered without hesitating.

"Maybe I'm not good enough for you."

"Good enough how? I don't think having a crappy ex makes you a bad person. That's on him," Caden told her, stroking her hair from her face.

She noticed he had a scrunchie around his wrist. Her daddy was getting her hair piled on her head, so it didn't get wet. He thought of everything.

"He is a bad guy," she agreed, loving the feel of his hands over her scalp. "I didn't mean that."

"Tell Daddy what's worrying you."

"I'm not anything special. I don't have big boobs or a badonkadonk."

Caden laughed at her term. "I'm not all smooth skin and white teeth, little girl. I've got scars and a couple of bullet holes Zale sewed up for me in the field. My body won't win a beauty contest. I hope that doesn't turn you off."

"Of course not. That's totally shallow."

Her words echoed in the silence of the empty room, making her consider what she'd said. "Oh! I don't think *you're* shallow."

"I'm glad to hear that, Brookie. I think you are beautiful, sexy, and utterly adorable. That won't change when I get your clothes off of you. It's a good thing we'll take Fluffikins into the bathroom as our chaperone or I might ravish you on the rug."

"Really?" she asked.

"Look at me, little girl."

It took her several seconds to meet his gaze fully. "Meeting you was the luckiest day of my life. I'm attracted to you on every level possible."

"Okay," she whispered. He'd never lied to her before. She'd gamble on trusting him now.

"Good girl. Now, before the tub overflows and sweeps the three of us out the front door, let's go pop you in the bath."

She nodded. Holding her bunny tightly to her chest, Brooklyn slid off his lap and wrapped her fingers around his. She followed him down the hallway and breathed a sigh of relief to see that the tub was only at the halfway mark. "We made it."

"We did. Are you ready to make your toughest decision of the day?"

"Maybe?"

He winked at her to reassure her. "Bubble gum or lavender scented foam?"

"Lavender tonight," she chose quickly.

"We'll both sleep like bugs in a rug then. Good choice." Caden picked up a purple plastic bottle and poured some of the fragrant mixture inside. Immediately, bubbles formed on the surface of the water.

"Quick! Let's get you inside the tub before there's no room for you."

Immediately, Brooklyn set Fluffikins on the vanity where he could see well. In the rush to get her clothes off, she almost forgot to be self-conscious. Caden did that on purpose, she thought as he helped her step safely into the tub. After a slight sting of discomfort when her punished bottom touched the warm water, she settled down in the fluff with a sigh of relief and enjoyment.

"The water feels heavenly."

"I'm glad, little girl."

Caden lifted a basket from the floor and selected several toys for her to play with during her bath. "Here's a mermaid and some floating flowers. Maybe a few seahorses and a squeezy clam?"

"Fun, Daddy!" She claimed the mermaid and swam her

through the water as he lowered himself easily to kneel next to the tub.

Busying herself with playing, she watched out of the corner of her eye as he grabbed a big blue pouf of netting and poured some thick liquid soap on it to bathe her. When he stroked it the length of her spine, she sat up straight with a sigh of delight.

"That feels incredible."

"Yay, Brookie. Thank you for letting Daddy know what you like."

As his washing caresses continued, she relaxed. This was amazing. Pure pampering.

"Let me steal this arm for a minute," he requested.

Her breath caught in her throat when the pouf brushed innocently along the sensitive side of her breast.

"You okay, Brookie?"

"Yes, Daddy." She daringly added, "That felt good."

"Let's see if I can find other delicious spots. Daddies love having a quest. And soldier daddies are the best trackers out there."

"Of all the daddies in the world?"

"Of course."

One of their first conversations replayed in her mind. "You told me you dated the neighbor of one of your teammate's Little."

"Yes. A few months ago."

"I didn't think through what you said. Your teammate has a Little?"

"I have three teammates with Littles. You'll get to meet them someday. We get together often."

"And there are six of you on the team? That's pretty wild odds that four of you are daddies," she said.

"The other two are daddies, too. Max and Hank haven't

found their Littles yet. Well, that's not true. Hank had a Little several years ago. She passed away."

"That's so sad." Tears prickled against her eyelids.

"It is. Now, I need a foot. Which one volunteers?" he asked, swooshing a hand around at the bottom of the tub. "Got one!" He pulled up the crab and looked at it as if he were completely baffled.

"That's not my foot!" she told him, giggling at his silliness.

"Thank goodness! I was a little scared, thinking your toenails felt like pincers!"

"Daddy, that's awful! Here's my foot. See! Perfectly normal toenails!"

He cupped her heel in his hand and checked her foot out carefully before washing her toes. "You're right! No pincers here."

She grabbed the crab floating on the surface and played with it. When Caden's hand stroked along the inside of her thigh, her hand tightened on the rubber object in her hand, and a stream of water arched toward her daddy's shirt.

"Sorry!" Brooklyn said quickly when a wet blob appeared on his T-shirt.

"I won't melt, Brookie," he reassured her and reached over his head to yank the soaked garment off.

Brooklyn almost choked on her tongue at the sight of Caden's muscles and the tattoos scattered over his broad chest. She was staring but couldn't stop. His raw power and handsomeness astounded her. Without thinking, she licked her lips.

"That will make my next set of four hundred push-ups totally worth it," he commented wryly.

"You can do that many?"

"On a good day," he teased. She had a hunch that meant he could do a ton more.

"I'm so out of shape."

"My job depends on my being ready to handle anything that comes my way. I don't expect you to do fifty pushups."

"Or two?" she asked, trying to sound like she was teasing but really being truthful.

"We might need to work on your being able to do two, little girl. You don't need to worry that we'll have a chin-up competition. I torture my team enough with physical training," he told her as he washed her other leg.

This time as he reached the top of her thigh, he swirled the pouf over her mound to her tummy. "Relax," he told her when she sucked in her gut.

"That's hard to do."

"You'll get used to me touching you, sweetheart." He swirled the soft fabric around her breasts and over her tightly clenched nipples.

Her eyelids drifted to half-mast as she focused on his movements. The almost physical sensation of his gaze watching her react to his caresses pushed her arousal higher. Brooklyn allowed the pleasure to erase her nervousness as she permitted her natural sensuality to take over. She arched her back, presenting herself for Caden's attentions.

"Very good, little girl. One more place to wash, and then Daddy will let you play for a few minutes before it's time for bed."

She squeezed her legs together, automatically guarding her most private area. Even sitting in the water, she could feel the slickness of her juices. The combination of being little in a bath of bubbles and his intimate touch seemed like a fantasy come true. Brooklyn couldn't believe her own daring. She'd never thought someone would make her secret dreams come true.

He stroked a hand from the base of her skull to a supportive spot between her shoulder blades and instructed, "Lean back on the tub and put your feet on the bottom."

After guiding her into position, he shifted her legs further apart. She didn't resist him. *Please. Let him touch me.*

A small moan slid through her lips as he stroked the pouf between her legs. Caden washed her pussy with a light pressure that made Brooklyn bite her lower lip to keep from begging. Still sensitive from his earlier caresses, she craved his direct touch—to feel his warmth instead of the netting. When he lifted her hips slightly while stabilizing her to whisk between her buttocks, Brooklyn slapped her hands over her face to hide. Watching him touch her was more intimate than hiding her face while she draped over his lap.

"No part of you will be off limits, little girl," he warned in a quiet tone that registered deeper in her jumbling thoughts than a loud voice.

"Yes, Daddy," escaped from her lips before she could stop it.

"Good girl. Now, you're all clean. You were such a good girl. Want to play for a bit or would you like to get out of the tub now and have time to get a special treat from your daddy?" Caden rose and looked down at her.

His response to bathing her caught her attention. His cock strained at the fly of his fatigues. Thrilled by his fierce reaction to touching her, Brooklyn almost forgot she needed to answer his question. "Treat!" she said quickly, wanting whatever he'd offer.

His low chuckle sounded wicked and hot, fueling the arousal inside her. Eager, Brooklyn shifted inside the tub, preparing to climb out to join him. To her surprise, he swooped forward and lifted her. Water streamed everywhere as her wet body pressed against his warm chest. Caden didn't appear to notice the mess.

Caden paused for a moment to admire her before setting her feet on the floor. The heat in his eyes reassured Brooklyn of his desire for her. As if forcing himself, he yanked a thick towel off the rack and dried her skin in quick movements that revealed his urgency. She loved that he allowed her to see his eagerness.

"Good enough," he muttered to himself and scooped her over his shoulder.

"Caden!" she yelped when his hand smacked her bottom.

"Just making sure you're paying attention," he told her and dipped his shoulder to toss her onto the bed.

By reflex, she grabbed a handful of the comforter. When the world stopped spinning, she focused on the handsome soldier standing between her legs in time to see him lower himself between her thighs. The hunger etched on his face almost stole her breath again.

He stopped her automatic move to draw her legs together. "Damn, little girl. You are gorgeous. Will you taste as good as you look?"

Caden leaned forward to trace her cleft and hummed with delight. The vibration rumbled her sensitive pink folds, thrilling her. "Daddy?"

"Such a good little girl choosing a treat. Now, both of us receive a reward." He spread her thighs widely and traced her opening with the point of his tongue before circling her clit.

She wiggled from a combination of embarrassment and eagerness. His caresses reignited her arousal. She'd never responded to anyone's touch as much as she did with him. Caden seemed to sense exactly where she needed his caresses, and how he needed to stimulate her.

When he slowly pushed two fingers deep into her pussy, Brooklyn lifted her hips to speed him up. She needed more.

"Daddy's in charge, Brookie," he growled against her.

His low, raspy voice revealed his desire, sending a thrill through her. Brooklyn loved knowing she affected him as much as he controlled her. "Treat, Daddy," she begged.

Caden's lips circled her clit and sucked. The pressure

grew as he slid his fingers deep inside. Brooklyn tensed and exploded into pleasure as that last bit of stimulation sparked her orgasm. She released the comforter to stroke a hand over his military-short hair when he stilled.

"Thank you. I could…" She let her voice trail away suggestively.

"Oh, I'm not done, sweetheart. That's a beginning."

Caden pressed his mouth back to her pussy. His lips and tongue tasted and caressed her. He even nibbled at her pink folds in a way that was so hot, she'd catch herself holding her breath and need to gasp for oxygen. When he trailed a fingertip to her small hidden opening between her buttocks, a wailing "No!" escaped from her lips.

"If you need me to stop, Brooklyn, tell me red. Otherwise, I'll know you're protesting something you think you should, but really want," he told her and paused for a second for her to respond.

"Sorry. I'm not used to someone touching me there," she explained.

"Red, Brookie, if you need me to stop," he told her and lowered his lips to rebuild her level of excitement as if he were completely unbothered by having to explain.

He's taking care of me even in the heat of passion.

She didn't have long to concentrate on that as he distracted her from logical thoughts. That feeling of being safe with him lingered to reassure her as he resumed touching the previously off-limits area. His fingertip brushed over her clenched opening, setting off zings of pleasure. When he pushed through that ring of muscles, another orgasm crashed over her.

He continued to pleasure her until Brooklyn draped limply on the bed. "No more, Daddy," she whispered and shivered from the avalanche of sensations as he pressed a kiss to her inner thigh.

"It's bedtime for little girls," he declared before asking, "Will you sleep with Daddy tonight?"

"Yes, please," she mumbled, not wishing to be separated from him.

Brooklyn couldn't open her heavy eyelids as he stood. Caden moved away from her. When the soft sheets brushed her skin lightly, she guessed he'd spread back the covers. When he returned to gather her in his arms and tuck her between the crisp sheets, she snuggled into the bedding. Burying her head in the pillow, she inhaled his scent. This was heaven.

His fingers brushed her hair from her face, and he kissed her lips softly. "Night, night, little girl. Daddy will be right back."

Hearing the shower start, she allowed herself to drift into sleep.

CHAPTER 8

Her twitching nose woke Brooklyn. Reaching a hand to her face, she rubbed her fingers over her skin to brush away whatever was tickling her. It didn't work. Opening one eye, she glared at the pesky intruder and froze. Chest hair.

Oh, my god! Brooklyn had somehow ended up smooshed to Caden's hard frame with her cheek resting on him. She took a second to savor his warmth and the powerful arm wrapped around her. Deliciously nude, Brooklyn could feel every inch of his warm skin pressing against her. This was heaven.

Forcing herself to shift several inches from him, Brooklyn gasped at the sound of Caden clearing his throat.

"Ahem. Stay where you are, little girl."

She tilted her head to meet his gaze. "Is everything okay?"

"Everything is better than okay. A precious little girl snuggled up to me last night within minutes of my returning from my shower."

"Oh, no. I'm sorry. I hope I didn't interrupt your sleep."

"I haven't slept this well in weeks, Brookie. I think I'll keep you."

"You think you'll keep me?" she repeated.

"With pleasure. Especially if I get a good morning kiss."

Before she could let her nerves stop her, Brooklyn stretched up to press her mouth to his. Caden took over immediately, rolling her backward to the pillows. His mouth captured hers and kissed her deeply. She clung to his shoulders, meeting his lips for each exchange.

When he finally lifted his head, she was panting. "It's official. You're mine." He patted her bottom, reigniting a slight sting from her spanking.

"I think I get some say in this decision," she said, teasing him.

"Shall I persuade you to agree with me?" he asked, grinning at her.

Brooklyn hesitated. She didn't want to disappoint him.

His hand stroking her hair back from her face drew Brooklyn from her thoughts. "Tell me what's going on in your head."

"You could have anyone. I'm no one special."

"Rule number one. You are not allowed to talk badly about yourself. That crappy ex obviously filled your head with a load of garbage. Probably because he has a small dick and puts others down to make himself feel better."

Her jaw dropped at his statement. Brent definitely had a much smaller penis than Caden had. Well, that she guessed Caden had. His steely erection had pressed against her hip when she'd sat in his lap. Brooklyn couldn't picture Caden as a man who would wear a sock in his fatigues.

Caden cupped her chin and lifted it back into place. "I'd say my suspicion was correct. Sweetheart, the world is full of people who only exist to torment others. We aren't those people. You are incredible, and I will never forget how lucky I am to have found you."

She searched his face. *Please don't let him be playing me!* To her delight, all she could see was Caden's inner strength and honor. "I think I was pretty lucky to find you too," she told him.

"Kiss me, little girl."

Pushing her worries and self-consciousness away, Brooklyn kissed him. Each brush of their lips illustrated how right he was for her. Like they were pieces of a puzzle that fit together perfectly. She ran her hands over his muscular chest, thrilled by the power and control her daddy had.

"Could you make love to me?" she whispered. Her cheeks blazed with heat as Brooklyn waited for his answer.

"Forever and a day," he answered, lowering his mouth to hers as his hands smoothed over her sides. Enjoying her nakedness, Caden caressed her. His hands hugged her curves, tantalizing Brooklyn.

When he pressed a line of kisses down the sensitive cord of her throat, Brooklyn tilted her head to invite Caden to explore. Butterfly brushes of his lips contrasted with his swirling tongue tasting her skin and his strong, white teeth nibbling a sizzling path. She never knew what would come next and wanted everything he offered.

Brooklyn squeezed her thighs together as her body responded to his touch. Eager to see and touch him, she pushed the covers off. She could feel the bumps and ridges of scars and injuries in addition to the rope-like muscles of his toned form. He was so handsome.

His hand glided over her stomach and up her ribcage to cup her breast. She shivered as he rubbed his work-rough thumb over her beaded nipple. Her nerves zinged with excitement at the slight abrasion. The warmth of his hand registered on Brooklyn seconds before he wrapped his lips around her taut peak, pulling it into the molten heat of his mouth. She arched her back, pushing her chest toward him.

Leaning back, Caden released her nipple with a pop of suction that surprised and titillated her. Was there anything that this man did that she didn't like? When he switched to her other nipple and rolled it gently between his teeth, she moaned with excitement.

She wanted to please him as well. Brooklyn glided her hands down his torso, tracing the muscles as they tensed under her fingertips. He reacted to her touch, his shaft jerking as she neared his pelvis. She loved having such an effect on him. Her fingers brushed his cock, drawing a deep groan from his throat. She wrapped her fingers around his shaft and gently squeezed.

"You are going to make me come faster than a teenager," Caden told her, sweeping her hand away.

"No fair. You get to touch me."

His gaze met hers directly. His blue eyes looked stormy, and his face was drawn with hunger. Seeing his arousal pushed hers higher.

"Brookie, I'll let you play all you want with Daddy's cock soon. This first time, I need to be buried deep in your heat."

She nodded eagerly. "Please."

"Let me make sure you're ready, sweetheart. Spread your legs for me."

Following his instructions immediately, Brooklyn inhaled sharply as he settled between her legs. That breath gushed from her lips as he drew a sizzling line down the center of her body to her mound. He ruffled her silky hair before tugging at it. She loved the slight bite of pain.

Caden trailed his fingers through her pink folds. "You're so wet, little girl. I think you're almost ready for Daddy to make you his."

"I'm ready," she assured him.

"One orgasm first, little girl. Can you come on Daddy's fingers?" he asked, caressing her intimately.

Her mind boggled as he targeted her most responsive spots he'd discovered last night. She only remembered them as he refreshed her memory, concentrating on those while seeking more. And she wanted everything.

Torn between focusing on the pleasure he coaxed from her and enjoying the delicious scenery he provided, Brooklyn savored the sensations and the view she could never have created in a fantasy. His chiseled frame loomed over her as Caden knelt between her thighs. Capturing her attention, his cock thrust upward, jutting away from his flat stomach. His form embodied power and masculinity that drew her on an instinctual level.

She stroked up the outside of his thighs. His crisp leg hair tickled her fingers, bringing a smile to her face as she remembered how amazing it was to wake up in his arms. *Please, let this be my life now.*

As if underlining her plea, Brooklyn catapulted into a massive orgasm that took her breath but left her feeling empty. She needed him to fill her. Lifting her pelvis toward him, Brooklyn begged, "Now, Daddy. Please."

His gaze met hers in a blaze of hunger and sexual heat. Caden leaned to the right and pulled open the nightstand drawer to grab a box of condoms. Roughly tearing it open, he quickly rolled the protection over his shaft as she devoured the intimate sight of his hands moving on himself.

She caressed his chest as he shifted over her. His heat radiated down to her as Caden placed the head of his cock at her entrance. Brooklyn closed her eyes, concentrating on the thrill of his thickness claiming her.

"Eyes on mine, little girl," he demanded in a voice rough with desire.

Instantly, she flipped her eyelids widely open to stare into his blue eyes. She felt like he could see into her soul. His mind and body connected with hers as he pressed inside her. She'd never be the same after this. Her fingers tightened on his ribcage as his thickness stretched her tight passage, igniting nerve endings along its path.

When she bit her lip, struggling to process the deluge of sensations, Caden paused instantly. "Brookie, are you okay?"

"Don't stop. I want it all," she whispered urgently.

"I don't want to hurt you, little girl. We're in no hurry. We have a lifetime together."

She clutched at him as he withdrew slightly. "No!"

"I'm not going anywhere, sweetheart. Let's try a different angle." Caden slid his hands under her hips and lifted her bottom off the mattress before gliding forward again.

"Oh!" she gasped as he slid fully inside her this time.

"Damn, Brooklyn. You feel so good wrapped around me."

His praise helped her relax, and he slipped a fraction deeper, drawing a groan from their throats. "Fuck. How could this get better?"

"Move?" she suggested with a slow wink. She gasped at a sharp sting. "You spanked me!"

"That was totally warranted, little girl. I can't wait to turn your bottom crimson. Hold on."

Before she could react, Caden withdrew and thrust deeply into her. She tightened her fingers on his torso as her eyes rolled back in her head with pleasure. She clung to him as he powered into her. Never giving her more than she could handle, he lavished a flurry of sensations on Brooklyn as he claimed her pussy.

Brooklyn loved his growling praise and groans as their bodies crashed together. Caden didn't hide anything from her but shared his pleasure freely. Their skin grew slick; heat gathered around them as they caressed each other. She loved the salty taste of his skin under her lips and the earthy sounds of their bodies moving against each other. Sex with Caden would never be civilized but raw and real.

Tingles gathered between her thighs, signaling her climax was close. "Daddy! Daddy, please."

"Come with Daddy," he ordered through gritted teeth. "Now!"

Quickening his thrusts, Caden pressed himself deep inside her. His face drawn with passion, he ground his pelvis to hers, providing that last bit of sensation that she needed. With a cry, she abandoned herself to an orgasm that rocked her body and mind. His muscles bunched under her fingers. With a roar that filled the room, Caden wrapped himself around her as he came.

CHAPTER 9

Many long minutes later, he held her curled up on his chest once again. Last night while sleeping, she'd moved close to him as soon as he'd returned from the shower. Her whisper of 'Daddy' had gone straight to his heart. Even in her dreams, she claimed him as hers.

Now holding her in his arms after claiming her, Caden would never let her go. His body's immediate reaction to her when they'd met at the guard shack told Caden to pay attention to this delectable woman. He didn't understand how his brain had figured out how special Brooklyn was. Thank goodness he hadn't questioned his gut instinct to protect her.

Brooklyn stirred. She propped herself up on one elbow to look at him as she wiggled. He loved the precious blush that appeared on her cheeks as their gazes met. "Are you okay, Brookie?"

She nodded and said, "Really happy. I've never felt like that before. You're good."

"We're good together, sweetheart."

"We are." Her gaze flittered past him, and Caden turned

his head to see what distracted her. Brooklyn focused on the clock. He read the numbers—eight o'clock.

"Don't you have to work today?" she asked, tensing.

"No, sweetheart. It's Saturday. I might just keep you in bed all day."

"I've totally lost track of the days," she confessed, shaking her head. "I'm glad we get to spend the day together."

"Me, too. Now, someone inspired me to quite a workout. I think I need a shower and food. What about you? Do you need to take a bath instead to soak away any soreness?"

The cute blush decorated her face, enchanting him. "I'm okay. But a shower is probably good." She stopped and sniffed her forearm. "I smell like you."

"I'm good with that."

"Caveman much?" she teased.

"With you around? Every moment of every day. I'm afraid I'm quite possessive of you. Does that bother you?"

She hesitated for a moment as if she were considering his question before answering. "No. It doesn't."

"I'm glad. Come on, little girl. Let's get cleaned up so we can have some breakfast. What's your favorite breakfast?"

"Waffles."

The speed in which she'd answered told him a lot. Waffles topped her list with several blank spaces below it. He didn't have a waffle maker. Caden grabbed his phone. "I need to ask my team for a favor," he explained to Brooklyn before texting.

RED ALERT. *Can anyone drop a waffle maker off on my doorstep in the next fifteen minutes?*

SECONDS LATER, Koa answered.

. . .

Little girls rock, don't they? Giana says you can borrow ours. She wants me to stress that it's just a loan.

You're a lifesaver, Koa. Thank Giana for me and tell her I'd never steal her waffle maker.

You can do that yourself. Barbecue at Zale's tonight. You're in charge of bringing dessert and the waffle maker.
Five p.m.?

Yes, sir!

"All set, little girl. Let's go shower. By the way, we are having a barbecue with the team and their partners. Would you like to see Giana again?"

"I'd love that. I didn't have a chance to say goodbye last time. You were so great at getting me out of the spotlight."

Caden got up and tugged Brooklyn out of bed. He tried not to let it go to his head when she swayed a bit on her feet. He loved that their lovemaking had knocked her a bit off balance. It certainly had impacted him inside. Wrapping an arm around her waist, he walked her into the bathroom and to the small separate room that held the toilet.

"Go potty, little girl."

Her quick dart inside told him everything. Her wiggles before they got up were a sign she needed to use the bathroom. Tucking her inside a diaper would prevent any accidents.

Caden turned on the shower to warm up and grabbed a couple of fresh towels to hang by the clear glass door. "I'm getting in the shower, little girl. Come join me when you finish."

"Yes, Daddy."

Stepping into the large, tiled shower, Caden celebrated his decision to enlarge the shower. Having extra room to accommodate two people easily was essential. He dunked his head under the spray and wet his hair. Quickly, he shampooed his hair. As he rinsed the suds, cool air wafted over his wet body.

"Hi, Brookie," he greeted her.

Her fingers stroked over his chest. He squinted one eye open to see her avidly ogling him. Caden reached out a hand to bring her close. "Hi, little girl. Are you ready to get clean?"

"Daddy! I'm getting wet," she protested, squirming against him.

She could have kept that motion up forever. His cock was automatically on alert.

"Daddy…" Her voice trailed off.

"Ignore my erection. I'm always going to get hard from the feel of your wet, gorgeous body wiggling on me."

"It's hard to ignore," she whispered.

"Concentrate on waffles," he suggested, turning so she stood in the stream of warm water.

He pumped the unscented gentle liquid soap into his hand. He spread the silky cleanser over her skin, enjoying caressing her. His little girl's moan of delight told him she enjoyed his efforts as well. She gasped as he slid his fingers through her pink folds.

"Sore?"

"No… Turned on," she admitted.

"That's a good thing. I know the feeling."

Her gaze returned immediately to his cock. "Can I touch you now?" she asked.

"How about if you help Daddy get clean?" Caden pumped the soap into her hand. Immediately, she focused on her task, spreading the cleanser over him as he attended to her.

Caden swallowed a laugh as her dedication to assisting him vanished. She simply drew a line down the center of his torso before wrapping her soapy hand around his shaft. Brooklyn carefully coated his cock with body wash and drew her hands one over the other, pulling on his shaft. Her first touch made his eyes roll back into his head—the second and third made him harder than stone.

"Brookie, I'm going to come all over you if you keep touching me like that," he warned.

"Mmm. Yes, please."

Her hands twisted slightly around him as she pulled on his cock. *Holy fuck!* Where did she learn that move?

He leaned his shoulders against the tiled shower wall for stability. Staring down his torso, he watched her hands move on his shaft. Caden couldn't decide what was more erotic—the sensations she created with her touch or the hot-as-hell visual he was devouring. As she threatened his control, he decided he didn't care.

She tilted her head to peek up at him. Caden had a split second to realize she was up to something before one of her hands lifted from his shaft to cradle his balls. He hadn't thought her caresses could get any better. Caden was wrong.

Brooklyn tugged gently at his sac, drawing a low moan from his lips. Three more drags of her hand over his cock and Caden was done. His cum splattered over her stomach, marking her in an animalistic way that registered deep inside him. She was his.

He pulled her to him and hugged Brooklyn close. She

pressed kisses to his skin as she clung to him. "Little girl. You're amazing. Thank you."

"That was fun," she whispered into his ear.

Caden closed his eyes, savoring her feather-light breath brushing him, like a physical caress to his highly sensitized skin.

"I'm glad you like to touch your daddy and make me feel good. I love to see you come."

"We're pretty perfect together, aren't we?" she asked, smiling up at him.

"We are."

Caden lifted her hand from his shoulder and checked out her fingertips. "Not to the prune-y stage yet. Let's get cleaned up. Waffles are waiting."

"I forgot!" she said, standing straighter.

"Let's rinse off, and we can see how fluffy our breakfast can be!"

CHAPTER 10

Brooklyn danced with excitement as Caden poured batter into the waffle maker they found waiting for them on the front porch. Caden loved her animated expressions as she chattered about what the waffle would look like.

"I wonder where they found this? I've never seen one shaped like a ladybug, Daddy! I wonder what other patterns they have? Do you think they have a bunny?"

"I don't know, sweetheart, but we can search for one," he told her.

"That would be so neat. I bet we could dye the batter and make the ladybug red. But how would we make the black spots?"

"Chocolate chips?"

She stared at him as if he'd cured cancer. "Yesssss! That would work! Do you have chocolate chips and red food coloring?"

He shook his head ruefully. "I'm sorry, little girl. I am woefully under-prepared to create colorful waffles."

"That's okay. We can see what kind of waffle iron we can

find. Then we'll get the stuff to jazz everything up." She paused for a moment, and the enthusiasm disappeared from her face. "I'm sorry. I shouldn't have made plans to spend money. I've got some. I can help pay."

"That won't happen. I have plenty of money to feed you and to buy a waffle iron. We won't buy six waffle irons, so you'll have to make sure you choose the best one."

"I don't like being a leech."

"You couldn't be a leech if you tried, little girl. How about if you let me worry about finances?"

"Do you promise you'll tell me if I become too much of a burden?"

Caden's heart skipped a beat. Her tone absolutely gutted him. He recognized then that her prior life contained more than an abusive ex who'd stalked her. The delicious scent of a waffle made him act quickly. He flipped the waffle off the griddle and onto a plate before addressing her request.

"Come to the table, Brookie. We'll eat this waffle while it's hot and talk."

"Am I in trouble? I didn't mean to offend you. Do you want me to leave?" she asked.

Hating the sight of the fat tears welling in her beautiful brown eyes, Caden wanted to nip this train of thought in the bud. "Come eat, little girl."

She slid off the stool at the island and followed him silently to the table. Caden cut a pat of butter from the stick and stabbed it with a fork before handing it to Brooklyn. "Here, baby. Rub this over the waffle. You can show me how much butter you like."

When she had taken the fork and pressed it to the golden creation, he calmly told her, "Good job, little girl. While you butter, I'm going to ask you some questions. Okay?"

"Sure," she said, looking up at him in concern.

"You are not in trouble. I'm trying to think of a scenario

where you would be or when I would ask you to leave. Maybe if you had an affair?"

"I'd never do that!" she exclaimed, forgetting her job and letting the butter melt on one section only.

Caden wrapped his hand around hers and guided the butter pat to another spot. "That's what I think, too. But if you fall in love with someone else, I'd hope you'd talk to me. May I explain my definition of a daddy?"

She nodded.

"A daddy is more than a passing relationship. It's not like having a boyfriend or girlfriend. For some, it's more than a husband or wife."

"More?" she repeated, puzzled.

"A more intimate relationship," he clarified.

"Oh! I guess I can see that."

"Is that enough butter?" he asked, checking out the puddles of melted butter pooling in the waffle's dents.

"Yes. But we need syrup."

"Of course we do. Tell me when," Caden said as he popped the top off the bottle. He poured until the waffle swam in the thick brown concoction.

"When, Daddy."

He stopped immediately and set the container down to cut her a bite. Holding it up to her mouth, Caden said, "Try this and see what you think."

"Mmm! This is the best waffle ever!" she mumbled around the bite. "You try it."

Caden helped himself to a sizeable chunk. It was over the top in sweetness for him, but this treat was for Brooklyn. He fed her another bite. "We did well. I didn't know ladybugs were so delicious."

"Daddy! It's not a real ladybug. That would be gross."

"Protein is protein, little girl."

She looked at him as if he'd grown another head. "Gross,

Daddy. Don't tell me you've eaten insects."

"Surviving is the most important. In many places in the world, bugs are a treat. Fried termites. Cricket flour. Human creativity nourishes a lot of people who would otherwise starve."

She studied the waffle suspiciously. "Cricket flour?"

"Your waffle is safe, sweetheart. I might sneak some veggies into lasagna, but I promise no insects in your food."

"Thank you."

"I can also promise you I won't kick you out. You're safe here."

"Is that because you're my daddy?" she asked.

"In part, yes. But even if you'd not had a little side, I would have welcomed you here. Years ago, I was in a bad spot. I haven't ever met my dad. My mom took care of me until my sixteenth birthday. That day, she decided I was grown enough, and her responsibility was over."

"That's horrible." Brooklyn bristled as she stiffened in outrage.

"It was. My possessions dwindled to what I could stuff in my hall and gym lockers. I slept on the wrestling mat in the back of the gym until the coach caught me."

"Oh, no! What did he say?"

"I thought on my feet and lied that I was there early to talk to him about being a wrestler. His expression alone told me that he didn't believe me, but he made me one of the team managers. That got me a key to the gym, where I could sleep and shower. There was even a washer and dryer that I could use overnight."

"He didn't take you home?"

"No, he was gay. Allegations that something fishy was going on could have cost him his job. I was fine. He made sure of that. I made it through high school graduation and joined the military. I've been there since."

"Do you like being in the military?" she asked.

"Yes. My team is my family."

"I really want to get to know them better now."

"They're going to be happy to spend time with you too. So I've told you my life story. Can you tell me yours while I make us another ladybug?" Caden asked.

"Let's call it a waffle, please. By the way, we aren't choosing an insect for our waffle iron."

He loved how Brooklyn had used the term *our*. It sounded like she planned to stick around. "Good idea." He stood and walked to the waffle iron to concoct another. Would she talk to him?

After a quiet pause as he prepared the griddle and poured the batter, Brooklyn said quietly, "My life was boring. I have parents who love me and were active in my life. I should have listened to their warnings when I met Brent. They picked up on something... Something off about Brent and his family long before I did."

"And you rebelled, ignoring their pleas for you to stay away from him?" Caden guessed. He could see this happening as if it were in real time. He forced the hatred he had for Brent into a controlled box inside him, so he wouldn't scare Brooklyn. No one threatened or manipulated his little girl. He closed the top of the waffle iron and walked back to her side.

"I was so stupid. Looking back now, I don't understand how I didn't pick up on the signs as well."

"You were young, and Brent was your rebellion." He smoothed a hand down her arm to reassure her. Brooklyn was not at fault here.

She shrugged. "You're too good at this. I wish I had been that perceptive. Anyway, Brent's family welcomed me. They were so nice in the beginning. Then they weren't. His family hasn't chased me for a while. Brent won't give up."

"I'm sorry, little girl. He won't bother you now."

"I don't want you to get hurt by him."

"I think I can take care of myself. And you, little girl. If not, I have an entire team of trained covert-military men who'll back me up."

"Hopefully, he'll decide to go back home now. Things can't be going well for him. He used to drive a fancy silver sports car. I noticed he was in a bashed-up blue car."

"It's hard to keep a job when you're harassing someone a couple of states away," Caden said.

"From what I hear from my parents, the word around our small town is that he's working as a day laborer now and living in that car. Unfortunately, he doesn't see that his crappy life results are from his decisions. Everything is always my fault. He hates me so much. It's scary."

Caden moved back to the griddle and rescued the golden waffle. "Round two. I vote we concentrate on this golden deliciousness and worry about Brent later. He's affected your life enough."

"Do you want to butter this one?" she asked, smiling up at him.

"No way. You're the expert."

Brooklyn concentrated on her task. Caden smiled as the tip of her tongue appeared at the corner of her mouth. Her life should always be this enchanting. He had to make this end for her. The team would help. They'd consider it a training exercise in handling urban threats.

CHAPTER 11

Brooklyn glanced at Caden as he drove toward Zale's. She'd woken up from the nap he'd insisted she take about an hour ago. Already, she had more energy than she had in a long time.

Caden reached a large hand over to wrap around her thigh when he noticed her looking at him. "You okay, Brookie?"

"Yes. I'm good. Better than good."

"Sounds like you need a naptime every day."

"I'm sure I'll get caught up on my sleep soon," she told him.

"Remember when I showed you the camera in that teddy bear on the tall dresser in your nursery? I'm going to check it at two p.m. each day. Your cute bottom better be in that crib or it will be red when I get home."

"You're not really going to spank me."

"Of course I am if you're naughty. If you don't fall asleep, you can read or simply relax, but I want you in bed from two to three."

Brooklyn bristled at his demands. Who was he to order

her around? She opened her mouth to argue, "Daddy…" That one word stopped her from arguing. If she wanted him to be her daddy, she should probably let him be one. Brooklyn rubbed her hand over his and smiled as he intertwined their fingers.

"Yes?" Caden asked.

"Never mind. I'll stretch out and try to nap."

"Good girl."

She squeezed his hand at the praise. Those two words did something to her inside.

They drove for a short time in silence until Caden slowed. Brooklyn leaned forward peering through the windshield. "There's a bunch of trucks there."

"We may be the last ones to arrive," Caden said.

"What if they don't like me?" Brooklyn asked.

"That's not going to happen. You helped save Giana, remember? Who knows what would have happened if you hadn't driven her away from that jerk."

"I don't want people to like me for that," Brooklyn admitted as he turned around to park in front of a small home.

"Even without that daring rescue move, everyone would love you. Just be yourself."

"All of the women with your teammates are Littles? I don't really know how to be little. What if I do something wrong?"

Turning off the car, Caden shifted in his seat to meet her gaze. "I'm sorry you're worrying so much. You seemed excited to go earlier. Do we need to leave?"

Brooklyn bit her bottom lip as she fretted over what to do. If they took off, everyone would think she didn't want to meet them. She did, but she was scared. The more she thought about it, the more her fear escalated.

A knock on the window made her shriek and jump. She

scrambled to the side, almost scaling the console that separated Brooklyn from her daddy. Caden scooped her into his arms and pulled her the rest of the way onto his lap.

"Sweetheart, you're okay. It's Giana. Look," he reassured her, pointing to Giana, who stood frozen outside.

"I'm sorry. I didn't mean to sneak up on you," Giana shouted through the glass.

"No, it's okay. I overreacted," Brooklyn panted, trying to stop shaking as she pressed herself to Caden's reassuring warmth. She'd forgotten to focus on her surroundings like she normally did.

"Giana, we'll come inside in a few minutes. Okay?" Caden called.

Giana nodded and appeared crushed. She jogged back inside. Brooklyn watched her go and suspected Giana was upset. Brooklyn's heart raced in her chest. She pressed a hand to her chest, trying to stop it.

"I feel horrible. She shouldn't blame herself for my being nervous. I shouldn't have panicked. You wouldn't let someone attack me."

"I wouldn't. I should have noticed Giana approaching. It's okay. We'll go in and you can talk to her in a couple of minutes. For now, let me hold you. Can you slow down your breathing? Inhale with me, sweetheart. Now, exhale."

Brooklyn struggled to follow his directions. Fortunately, after a few rounds, she could match her breath to Caden's. The panicky feelings inside her chest lessened, and she relaxed against him.

"Feeling better, Brookie?"

"Yes, thank you."

Caden kissed her temple and hugged her close. "Would you like to go inside, or should I call Zale and tell him we needed to go home?"

"We have the dessert. They'll hate us if we don't take it in."

"They won't hate us, but that's a good excuse to join everyone. I think Giana would like to see that you're okay," Caden told her.

Brooklyn hesitated and then agreed. "You're right. We need to go inside. If I give you a sign, will you get me out of there?"

"You bet." Caden popped open his door before she could change her mind. He carried her with him as he stepped out. Setting her feet on the street, he wrapped his arm around Brooklyn's waist until she was steady. "That's my girl. Shall I get the dessert and the waffle maker?"

She nodded and stood quietly, scanning the area as he shifted to grab the stuff in the back. When he returned to her side, Brooklyn tucked herself next to him. Caden pressed a hand to her lower back and guided her around the house to the backyard.

"Hi, everybody," he called.

Greetings came to them from the small groupings. Three men stood by the grill, flipping burgers. Giana sat with two other women on lawn chairs nearby. The final two men played a game with targets and beanbags. Zale headed forward to greet them.

"Hi. I'm glad to see you again, Brooklyn. Welcome!. Please make yourself at home." A brunette appeared beside him. "Here's Pippa. She's my little girl."

"Brooklyn, I'm so glad to meet you. Thank you for helping Giana," Pippa told her as the other women joined their conversation.

Brooklyn stiffened her legs to keep from running. "Hi, Pippa. Zale. I'm afraid I made a fool of myself outside. I'm sorry, Giana."

"Oh, no! I was an idiot. I dealt with a threat for a short time, and I still freak out from time to time from something random. I'm really sorry I scared you," Giana told her with tear-filled eyes. "Especially after you saved me."

Brooklyn stepped away from Caden and wrapped her arms around Giana. "How about if we forget we saw each other a few minutes ago? I'm really glad to know that you're safe now."

"I'd like that. Let me introduce you to Aspen." Giana stepped back slightly to wave the other young woman forward. "This is Aspen."

"Hi, I'm Brooklyn."

"Hi! We're glad you're here," Aspen greeted her cheerfully.

"Giana told us about you driving like a badass to get her to the base," Pippa said with a grin.

"Language, Pippa!" Zale corrected from behind the cluster of women.

"Sorry, Daddy," Pippa apologized. She turned back to the women to whisper, "I've already gotten in trouble twice today. Let's go talk over there by the swings."

Giana hooked her arm with Brooklyn and said, "Good idea."

The quartet distanced themselves together. Brooklyn couldn't believe how the conspiracy to keep the men from overhearing their conversation made her feel like one of the group immediately. She glanced over her shoulder at Caden and gave him a thumbs up. He smiled and waved.

"Are you really okay?" Giana asked quietly.

"Just jumpy. I'm always expecting the worst to get me."

"I hate that for you. You're safe here. Those guys would take down anyone who even thought of messing with us," Giana told her in a louder voice that the other women could hear.

As the others nodded, Giana added, "I'm strong. I'll keep you safe as well."

A movement caught Brooklyn's eye, and she looked past

the ladies to see an enormous animal approaching. "Um... Is that beast friendly?"

The massive dog bumped into Aspen's leg and leaned his heavy bulk on her. Everyone laughed as Aspen took a step to the side before bracing her legs to withstand the weight. "This is Rexy. Despite his fierce appearance, he's a big softie."

"He has to eat a lot," Brooklyn said, studying Rexy.

"He does." Aspen winked at her. "He's handy for munching the green beans I don't want to eat. Rexy draws the line at broccoli, unfortunately."

"Suddenly, I want a dog," Brooklyn said.

"I know. Right?" Giana chimed in. "I work long shifts. It wouldn't be fair for a dog to be trapped inside for so long. I have to eat my own vegetables."

"Daddy approaching!" a voice warned.

The women turned to see Zale heading their way. Brooklyn realized he'd announced his arrival so she wouldn't get spooked. She really appreciated his thoughtfulness.

"It's dinnertime. Come grab a burger. There might even be some *veggies* for you to eat." Zale met at each little girl's eyes to make sure they'd gotten his message.

"No fair using your supersonic hearing, Daddy," Aspen fussed before turning to Rexy. "And you! Why didn't you warn us?"

"We sent him down to tell you to come eat. You didn't read the note I tucked under his collar," Zale said.

Aspen ran her fingers around Rexy's neck and pulled out an empty plastic bun bag. She held it up and glanced up at her daddy. "I don't get it."

"Doesn't that say the hamburgers are ready?" Zale asked, chuckling.

The women spontaneously groaned in unison.

"We couldn't coordinate our reaction to the bun message

again if we tried," Pippa said. The group dissolved into giggles.

"If we don't get up there soon, Max will eat all the food," Zale told them.

Max's piled-high plate immediately motivated everyone. Caden's plate looked very similar a few minutes later. Of course, he'd piled food on his to feed both of them. Brooklyn settled happily on his lap like the other Littles did with their daddies.

I wish this moment could last forever. Brooklyn hadn't enjoyed a social life since Brent got mad at one of her friends after another and shut them out of her life. Brooklyn could feel the ties between the men. They would be friends for a long time after their military service ended. Brooklyn basked in the laughter and good-natured ribbing that characterized the group's interactions.

She also learned a lot about her daddy. These powerful, skilled men trusted Caden with their lives. In return, he had dedicated himself to making sure each soldier was battle-honed and prepared to survive whatever the higher-ups threw at them.

Caden had never talked about his efforts with the group. He'd never bragged about himself or taken credit for the team's successes. Her heart bursting with pride, Brooklyn kissed his cheek.

"Are you okay, sweetheart? Was that a signal that we need to leave?" Caden asked.

"No way. This is fun. Thank you for bringing me, Daddy."

"Super fabulous!" Pippa called, holding one of the fudgy brownies Brooklyn had chosen for her and Caden to bring for dessert. "These are amazing!"

"I think the brownies were a good choice, little girl," Caden whispered in her ear. "Want to go get us one before they disappear?"

Nodding, Brooklyn slid off his lap to dart over to the picnic table. The debate over caramel or double-chocolate brownies being the best completely distracted her from returning with a brownie. The women slid onto the bench seats and chatted, enjoying the chocolaty treats that seemed to evaporate before their eyes.

"You didn't save me one, did you, little girl?" Caden asked from the end of the table.

Brooklyn looked at the empty platter and felt bad. "Oops? Sorry, Daddy."

Caden patted his flat abdomen like he was Santa with a big belly. He turned slightly back to the men and announced in a loud voice, "That's okay, Brookie. I'll have less to burn off tomorrow in our ten-mile training run."

"I should not have eaten that second helping of potato salad," Koa moaned.

Laughter filled the backyard. Happy, Brooklyn stood and rushed to hug her daddy. *If only this could last.*

CHAPTER 12

*E*nchanted by her sweet face, Caden allowed himself to stay in bed for several long minutes to watch Brooklyn sleep. Having her here was a dream come true. Sure, there were complications, like her panic last night, but when didn't a relationship have a few bumps? He couldn't believe he had fallen so hard and so fast, but here he was in love with this incredible woman.

"Mmm," she murmured and rubbed her cheek on the pillow.

Caden eased himself away, wanting her to sleep in much later than his internal clock had alerted him. He held his breath as he pulled a drawer open a couple of inches to grab a pair of sleep pants. After pausing at the door to glance back at the adorable sight of her holding her bunny under her chin, Caden quietly closed the door before stepping into the garment he held.

Soon, he sat on the couch, scrolling through his phone as he drank a glass of milk. Caden didn't own a coffeemaker. He didn't see the point in one. A brisk run woke him up much faster than caffeine.

The sun shone brightly into the room when he checked the clock again, wondering how long she would sleep. A quiet yawn drew his attention to the hallway. Brooklyn stood framed in the opening with the comforter wrapped around her like an oversized hoodie. Caden tossed his phone onto the end table and opened his arms.

"Come here, Brookie."

She walked slowly over to him and climbed onto his lap. "Daddy, you left me in bed."

"You and Fluffikins were sleeping so well. I didn't want to wake you."

"I missed you."

"That's so sweet. I missed you too. We have the whole day together. What shall we do? There's a great zoo here in town. I could give you a tour of the base. Maybe you'd rather go shopping?"

"I'd love to see the base, but I'd rather do something else," she whispered, peeking up at him.

"Okay. What would you like to do?"

"The girls said they have pacifiers…"

Caden smiled at her. He loved that she had enjoyed her time with the other Littles. Brooklyn had obviously decided that she was comfortable talking to them. Caden would have to thank Aspen, Pippa, and Giana for welcoming his Little.

"I have some in your nursery. Shall I go grab one for you?"

"Okay…"

Something in her tone told him he wasn't understanding her. Did she not want a pacifier? "You had something else in mind?"

"Um…"

"You can tell me anything, little girl. What's wrong?"

"Can I suck on your cock?" she blurted.

Instantly, his shaft twitched and stiffened. "Daddy would love to feel your mouth wrapped around my cock, Brookie."

She wiggled against him, drawing a groan from his lips when her full bottom rubbed his growing erection. He reached out to wrap his hands around her waist, steadying her.

Brooklyn studied him with a puzzled expression. "Daddy, I can't get on my knees if you're holding on to me. Here. You hold Fluffikins."

He accepted the stuffed bunny that she handed him. To his delight, she sank to the floor in front of him. Shrugging her shoulders, she dropped the comforter back to the floor to reveal her beautifully nude form. Caden clamped down on his arousal as the sight of his temptress. Brooklyn ran her hands over his inner thighs and tugged his tented sleep pants tight.

"Take these off," she demanded, untying the thin garment and looking at him as if he wasn't following the rules for blowjobs.

Caden elected not to ask questions. He lifted his hips and pushed the thin material down. Brooklyn tugged them to his ankles and unlooped the fabric from around one foot. She pushed his legs apart and settled between them. Caden forced himself to breathe as he mentally thanked whoever had created the process Brooklyn followed.

I need to read her romance novels.

Her gaze felt physical as she scanned his body. She reached out to rub her hands over his stomach. Caden didn't think he could get any harder as her fingers inched closer to his cock. He scooted his hips down to the edge of the couch to encourage her.

"Thank you, Daddy," she said politely and trailed her fingers through his pubic hair. When she tugged at a few of the strands, Caden knew he was in trouble.

"Little girl…" Words disappeared from his brain when she leaned forward to lick from the base of his jutting shaft to the tip. Light flicks of her fingernails followed that trail as Brooklyn opened her lips to exhale a hot stream of air over his now damp cock. A split second later, her mouth surrounded him, and her hand wrapped around his shaft to hold his erection steady.

Caden's hands tightened around the soft fur of the bunny in his hands. His one last functional brain cell warned him not to harm the stuffie. He set it on the cushion next to him and grabbed the edge of the couch seat as she sucked on his cock as if it were the pacifier she'd mentioned earlier.

Her sweet sounds of enjoyment rocked him as she swirled her tongue over his skin. Her fingers squeezed him at different intervals, keeping him on edge and unable to anticipate what she would do next. Caden's eyes rolled back in his head when she dipped her head closer, taking him deeper into her throat.

"Baby," he whispered, forcing his hand from the cushion to brush the hair back from her face. He needed to see everything. "That's so good."

She hummed around his shaft. The vibration pushed his arousal even higher. He wouldn't last long. That amazing mouth would quickly defeat his control.

Air gusted from his lips as she traced one fingertip down to his balls. Like an abstract artist, she drew a pattern on the tightly wound globes. Just when he thought he'd lose it, Brooklyn pressed her finger to that small space between his sac and his clenched opening.

With a roar, Caden drove his hips forward as he emptied himself into the heat of her mouth. Brooklyn continued to caress him until he collapsed back on the couch. Caden lifted his arms toward her.

"Come here, little girl. I need to hold you."

Moving carefully, she straddled his pelvis and allowed Caden to pull her down on his chest. "Did I do good, Daddy?"

"No, sweetheart. You totally blew my mind. That's way beyond good. I'd rate that as phenomenal."

"I loved tasting you."

He thought she'd burned out all his arousal energy. That four-word sentence revived him. "You did, hmmm?"

She licked her lips. A picture of her sucking on a pacifier popped into his mind. He had to get his little girl a pretty pacifier. Watching her mouth move on it would always remind him of the first time she'd requested to give him a blowjob.

"Daddy, do you think you could grow to love me? You know, the real kind of love that lasts for years?"

He leaned forward to kiss her hard, showing her the emotions inside him—passion, caring, and most of all, love. When he lifted his mouth from hers, Brooklyn lifted a shaking hand to press her fingers to her lips.

"Brooklyn, I don't have to think about tumbling head over heels for you. You've already carved a spot in my heart. I love you, sweetheart."

"Really?" she whispered, searching his face as if to ensure he wasn't making something up. A tear rolled down her cheek, and he kissed it away.

"I think you stole my heart when I met you on base. You were petrified, but you'd stepped in to help a stranger."

"I know what it's like to have a predator after you and be alone."

"You aren't alone anymore, little girl." He wondered if she would be brave enough to tell him that she loved him. Caden didn't doubt that she cared deeply for him as well. Their connection was too strong for her to feel any other way.

"Thank you for loving me, Daddy. I... I need to tell you something," she confessed.

A flare of panic zinged through him. Had he misunderstood her reaction to him? He could see the concern etched on her face. "You're safe here, little girl. You can tell me anything." Mentally, he crossed his fingers. Caden would be crushed if she chose to stay with him simply to remain safe from Brent.

"I knew you loved me. My heart told me you did."

"How did your heart share that news?" he asked, completely charmed.

"Your heart beats slowly and steadily. When I'm with you, my heart tries to match yours. If I'm close to you, our heartbeats synchronize. You try." She grabbed his hand and pressed it between her breasts.

Focused on his hand, Caden waited for her heart to settle after her motion. His gaze rebounded to her face after a short time. "That's amazing. How did you ever notice this?"

"Because my heart goes pitter-patter when I see you. Then when I'm in your arms, it either goes crazy," she waggled her eyebrows suggestively, "or it gets calm. I think my heart has decided I'm safe with you."

That last statement told him all he needed. Brent had made her life hell for way too long. "I'm glad you're happy with me, little girl."

"More than happy. Being with you feels right for the first time. I love you too, Daddy."

Caden cupped her face with his hand and drew her lips to his. He kissed her with the love in his heart, and her pulse quickened. Drawing back slightly, he whispered, "I'll need you to tell me you love me a lot, Brookie."

"A thousand times a day," she promised.

"That might be enough." Caden hugged her close. How had he gotten so lucky to find Brooklyn?

CHAPTER 13

"Not fucking now," Caden cursed under his breath when his phone blared a loud alarm. Answering the call, he said, "Got it, Jerico. See you in fifteen." He rolled out of bed and grabbed a duffel bag from the closet.

"What's that?" Brooklyn asked, propping herself up on one elbow. Being jerked out of a deep sleep had completely disoriented her. Almost immediately, she realized what had happened. "That's the alert you told me about?"

"Yes, sweetheart. They've activated the team. Jerico's going to pick me up soon. Come talk to me while I shower."

Brooklyn wrapped the comforter around her nudity and followed him. Caden hadn't waited for the water to warm. He already stood under the spray, rinsing off the traces of their lovemaking. "Do you have to go?"

"Yes, Brookie. This is my job, sweetheart," he told her before dunking his head under the showerhead. When he emerged, he shook his head and continued, "Drive my truck while I'm gone. That way Brent won't recognize your car."

"I won't go anywhere," she rushed to reassure him as he

stepped out to dry off after the quickest shower she'd ever seen.

Caden dried himself off with rough swipes of the towel. "I don't know how long I'll be gone, little girl. You may need to get some supplies. Remember that I have the emergency credit card in the drawer. You're okayed to use it. You can order food, too, through the app we put on your phone."

"There's a lot of food in the kitchen. Do you think you'll be gone that long?" Brooklyn's stomach rolled at the thought of being without him for a long time.

"When I get on base, they'll share intel with the team. Sometimes, the mission is a quick in-and-out task, and I could be back in a couple of days. Everything can change rapidly. Depending on how things go, it could be fast or extended."

He threw the towel in the laundry hamper and walked forward to hug her tightly to him. "I need you to stay safe. You have the base emergency line if anything happens, and I put Brent's case number on the fridge if you need to call the police. Remind them of that incident if anything suspicious spooks you."

"I have the other Littles' phone numbers as well," she said.

"Good. Keep your phone charged and with you."

"Yes, Daddy. I love you." Brooklyn wanted to make sure he heard and remembered that.

"And I love you, little girl."

He kissed her hard before taking her hand and leading Brooklyn back into the bedroom. She sat on the bed as he pulled on his military fatigues.

Will I see him again? Her heart broke at that thought. She brushed away a tear to keep him from seeing her upset. Caden needed to focus on the mission—not worry about her.

He held out his hand when he finished to tug her off the bed. Caden squeezed her hand as they walked down the hallway. They'd reached the family room when headlights rolled over the ceiling, signaling that a vehicle had parked in the driveway.

"That's my ride, Brookie. Take care of yourself for Daddy. It's okay to be sad, but remember that I will do everything in my power to get back to you as quickly as possible. I just found you. I have more to live for now than ever before. Okay?"

"Yes, Daddy. I'll miss you so much."

Caden kissed her hard before swatting her behind sharply. "I'm going to spank this bottom when I get back," he promised.

"I'm going to hold you to that," she said, trying to maintain her composure.

After another hard kiss, Caden told her, "Look in the pantry tomorrow," and he was gone.

Brooklyn slid down the wall in the dark room and cried until her chest hurt and her tears had dried up. Forcing herself to stand, she walked back to the bathroom to pull his towel out of the hamper. She pressed it to her nose and inhaled, savoring his scent clinging to the fabric. Carefully, she folded the towel and hung it on the rack before heading back to their bed to curl up on his pillow with Fluffikins. Even her stuffie couldn't console her.

Sure she wouldn't sleep anymore, Brooklyn filled her mind with memories of spending time with her daddy. When she jerked awake several hours later to her surprise, the bedroom was full of light. Caden had to be far away by then. She hugged herself and sent love after him. Her heart rate settled into his slow pattern, putting a smile on her face. He'd gotten the message.

"Fluffikins, we need to do something today. Let's start with breakfast."

She got up and dressed slowly. It was going to be a long

day. She might as well not rush. Hurrying would create more time for her to fill. Before leaving the bedroom, Brooklyn hugged Caden's pillow. Its squishiness didn't substitute for squeezing his hard body.

In the kitchen, she paused to consider what to have for breakfast. Her phone rang on the charger in the kitchen. Daddy always plugged it in there because he didn't want her sleep to be disturbed. Jumping to her feet, Brooklyn ran to the counter to check the display. It wasn't Caden.

"Hi, Aspen."

"You sound disappointed," the sweet woman said.

"I'm sorry. I thought maybe it would be Daddy."

"Of course you did. I'd be worried if you didn't sound unhappy that it was me calling," Aspen teased. "Are you doing okay?"

"I wasn't scared when my daddy was here. Now, I'm jumping at every sound again."

"Have you heard anything from Brent?" Aspen asked. Her tone sounded sharper, like she was concerned.

"No. Nothing. It's all in my mind," Brooklyn confessed.

"That's easy to understand. You've been through a lot. When I want to distract myself, I plan how I'm going to welcome my daddy home. I try on different outfits and practice my seduction moves in front of the mirror."

"No way! You are so bad, Aspen!"

"So bad I'm good," Aspen said, and Brooklyn could picture the grin on her friend's face as Aspen continued, "Rexy looks at me like I'm a dork and goes to sleep somewhere, but I have fun. You could try it too."

Caden's blue eyes dark with arousal flashed into her mind. Could she seduce him? Brooklyn was confident her daddy would enjoy any plans she created. A flashback to him making sweet love to her when she'd woken up from a bad dream popped into her mind. Whatever he was doing had to be dangerous. Maybe she could distract him from the monsters that lived in his thoughts.

"Earth to Brooklyn. Stop thinking about your daddy's fancy sex moves." Aspen's giggles danced through the phone lines. Brooklyn joined in her merriment, allowing her friend to lighten her mood.

A few seconds later, the reality of her daddy's absence flooded back, making her sad. Aspen had distracted her once. Brooklyn guessed she had more ideas. "What else do you do when your daddy is gone, Aspen?"

"I miss him," Aspen told her honestly. "It helps to get together with Giana and Pippa. We'll call you when we make plans."

"Thank you. Maybe I can join you by phone at least. I'm going to avoid being seen. I'm sure Brent is still out there somewhere."

"We'll come to you then. Maybe have a sleepover?" Aspen suggested.

"I'd love that. Check your schedules and tell me when you're free. I'll order some fun snacks."

"We'll bring stuff. If we all share something we love, we'll have too much," Aspen told her. "That always happens at parties. I'll ask what date works for everyone."

"Thanks, Aspen." Brooklyn hesitated for a minute before asking, "Is it okay to call you if I have a question or get lonely?"

"You bet. I've already called you because I miss my daddy so much. You cheered me up and gave me a project to work on."

A couple of minutes later, Aspen excused herself to take Rexy out to potty. Almost instantly, Brooklyn's phone buzzed with an incoming message. Aspen had set up a chat. She'd given it the name SDL. Soldier Daddies' Littles.

The rest of that day crept by. Caden had told her to check

in the pantry, but Brooklyn ate the food in the refrigerator first since it could go bad. She watched a couple of movies and played in her nursery. She even took a nap to make the day go faster. When shadows finally filled the interior again, Brooklyn borrowed a book from the stack under an end table in the family room and curled up in her daddy's bed.

She was eager to explore books that her daddy enjoyed. Maybe she'd learn something new about him. The thriller pulled her into the story instantly. Brooklyn wasn't a fast reader, but she loved losing herself in a wonderful novel.

To her delight, she woke up the next morning with the book lying next to her on the bed. She'd survived one night without her daddy. Hopefully, he would come home soon.

The days passed slowly. Brooklyn was used to hiding inside, but that didn't mean she enjoyed it. Now after having Caden around, crushing loneliness hit her harder than it ever had before.

She explored the things in her nursery. When the pacifier he'd unwrapped for her had helped her nap one afternoon, Brooklyn dared to check out the other supplies in the changing table. The sight of the thick thermometer and the lubricant sent a thrill through her. The case had the word RECTAL in big red letters. Could she let Caden take such intimate care of her?

As Brooklyn closed the drawer, her knee knocked one of the folded diapers off the bottom shelf. She'd looked at them from a distance but never had checked one out closely. Having Fluffikins in her arms boosted her bravery. Brooklyn opened the padded garment and pushed at the cushiony material. She checked out how it would fit around her. Did people actually pee in this? It didn't seem as thick as she'd expect it to be. Surely, a Little would have an accident?

Brooklyn squeezed her legs together. Her panties were soaked. Before she could talk herself out of it, she yanked off her leggings and underwear. Fumbling, she fitted the diaper around her body. The crinkling sound made her feel littler than she'd ever experienced before.

She almost yanked it off, frightened by the level of emotion the diaper created. Forcing herself to take this chance to experience everything, Brooklyn plopped down on her padded bottom. She loved the faint scratch of the gathered diaper around her waist and legs. Each sound and sensation reminded her it was okay to be little.

A familiar fantasy of her daddy lifting her to the top of the changing pad popped into her mind. He'd wrap that belt around her waist to prevent her from rolling off. Other restraints popped from one side. Those had to allow her daddy to tie her hands above her head.

Brooklyn rubbed the front of her diaper as she imagined her daddy taking care of her so intimately when he'd tethered her in place. They'd discussed experimenting with all levels of age play. The padding lessened the sensation of her strokes. Frustrated, Brooklyn laid back and thrust her hand inside the diaper.

Sliding her fingers through her slick juices, Brooklyn caressed her pink folds. She bit her lower lip as she brushed her clit. Returning to the small bundle of nerves, she pushed her arousal higher until her hips rose from the carpet. Crying out, Brooklyn climaxed strongly—so fiercely that she squirted into the padding of the diaper. Slumping back on the soft flooring, Brooklyn tried to catch her breath.

"Daddy. Come home. I want you to take care of me," she whispered into the now quiet nursery.

CHAPTER 14

When the fresh food in the refrigerator had dwindled to a few apples and random staples like teriyaki sauce and mustard, Brooklyn debated what to eat that morning for breakfast. Remembering his treat for her at that first meal of apples and peanut butter, she headed for the pantry to grab the jar. "Oh, yeah, Fluffikins. Daddy told me to look in the pantry."

She opened the door and froze. Inside was a large box with several smaller boxes stacked on top. Each was wrapped in different festive paper—birthday, Christmas, baby, Valentine's Day, and turquoise blue. He'd remembered her favorite color!

How had Caden stashed these in here without her seeing? She tugged the pile out into the kitchen and sat on the floor. Was she supposed to open everything now? "He's not going to be gone for all the holidays, is he?" Brooklyn asked Fluffikins, trying not to cry at that thought.

To cheer herself up, Brooklyn took a picture of her presents and posted it in the group chat with the other Littles. Excited comments followed as everyone demanded to know what she found inside. When she shared she hadn't opened any, Pippa encouraged her to dive in. Giana wanted her to open the smallest one first and build up to the largest. She decided to do as Aspen suggested and to open one present a day.

After a long debate, Brooklyn chose the largest package. She carefully peeled the paper off, trying not to tear it. Some letters appeared as the paper sagged away from the box. LL HOU.

"It can't be," she said out loud.

Brooklyn threw neatness into the wind and ripped the paper ferociously until the picture on the front appeared. It was an enormous dollhouse. She made herself take a minute and snap a picture of the box and send it to her new friends. Then she ignored the buzzing incoming messages to open the gift.

Carefully pulling out the parts, Brooklyn celebrated everything. Soon the floor was littered with furniture, miniature figurines, walls, roof and floor sections, and even small details like curtains, rugs, and hangers. When she found the directions, Brooklyn forced herself to stop and read them through. She really wanted to throw herself into the construction and figure it out as she went, but this was too important. She wanted it to turn out perfect.

It came with miniature tools to put things together. Brooklyn leapt to her feet and ran to the kitchen to get a plastic bag to store them. The direction booklet had ten pages. Brooklyn decided to complete half today and half tomorrow. That would give her something to do for two days.

Carefully, she read the first step and dived in. An hour later, she finished fitting together what she had allotted for today. Eyeing the project, Brooklyn struggled with the temptation to finish it. The middle floor was a bit wobbly. She couldn't leave it like that. Maybe it would be better to complete all the pages and then tomorrow, she could work on the furniture and décor.

Afternoon shadows filled the house as she placed the last rug on the floor in front of the fireplace. The dollhouse was exquisite. Brooklyn sent thank-you vibes to her daddy. She took another picture and sent it to the chat.

To her astonishment, Brooklyn scrolled back and guesstimated the other Littles had sent over a hundred messages. What had she missed? Scanning them quickly, she watched new ones pop up.

Giana: Six hours! I win!

Pippa: It was closer to seven. That makes Aspen the best guesser.

Aspen: Both of our guesses were so close. I vote we share the prize.

Brooklyn: What prize? And you were betting on how long it would take me?

Pippa: I guessed ninety minutes. I obviously have never constructed a dollhouse, but that was a ton of pieces!

Aspen: It's gorgeous! I want to come play!

Pippa: Count me in! Tomorrow? I'm off at six. If you all want to order pizza, I'll pick it up on my way over.

Giana: I can make it then. I'm off tomorrow. Well, unless there's an emergency.

Aspen: I'll bring dessert. Don't worry about anything, Brooklyn. We'll come prepared.

Giana: I've got drinks.

Brooklyn: I can do something.

Pippa: You're sharing your present with us and hosting.

Brooklyn: Okay! See you tomorrow.

Wrapping her arms around herself, Brooklyn gave herself a hug. What had started out as another tough day had become one of the best. Her daddy had done this for her. She turned to consider the stack of presents still waiting to be opened and shook her head. This one was enough. She would save the others for the next time he was gone.

Brooklyn walked into the pantry and scanned the shelves, spotting a lot of space at the top. She could put them there out of the way. It was too high for her to reach, so she pulled a chair close and lifted one package before stepping onto the seat. One by one, she set them safely on the shelf.

The final one wavered a bit on the edge. Brooklyn took her time to balance it. *There! That's it!*

She held on to the lower level as she returned to the floor. *Oh, no!*

Brooklyn made a wild grab for the package as it tumbled. Her foot hit one of the chair legs, sending her off balance. The tiled floor seemed to rush up to greet her with dizzying speed. A brief flash of light and pain hit her before darkness took her.

"Ow!" Brooklyn lifted a hand to her head and immediately slowed her movement as her vision swam. When she finally pressed against the spot that hurt, her fingers touched wet and sticky hair. Had she fallen into water? Reversing the process, the sight of blood coating her skin made her stomach heave.

She struggled to think clearly as she stared in horror at her hand. A pulsing headache pounded inside her skull, making it tough for her to think. She needed help. What should she do? What *could* she do?

Call someone.

Brooklyn carefully shifted a hand to her pocket. The familiar ridge of her device was gone. Where had she left it? Looking up, she tried to think. Everything was hazy. Was that a black ridge hanging over the middle shelf? Suddenly she remembered setting her phone down there to carry in the packages. Pushing her elbow into the cold flooring, she attempted to sit up and froze when another wave of nausea cascaded over her.

When she regained control, Brooklyn looked around with her eyes to avoid moving her head. Nothing. She moved her arms slowly to search by touch. Refusing to dwell on the scary amount of wetness around her, Brooklyn focused only on her goal. She had to reach her phone. Panicking now wouldn't help her.

Her fingers closed around a broom handle in the corner. Bringing it in front of her, Brooklyn knocked the phone off the shelf. A gasp of pain burst from her mouth as the corner of the device landed sharply on her right breast. Dismissing the impact as incomparable to her headache, Brooklyn fumbled with her phone.

The chat window appeared on the screen, and she pushed the phone icon. *Please let someone answer.*

"Brooklyn? You couldn't wait to talk to us?"

"Giana! I'm sorry to call, but I need help."

"What's wrong?" Her friend's voice immediately changed from friendly to emergency responder efficient.

"Brooklyn? What's up?" Aspen asked, joining the call.

"Quiet!" Giana demanded. "Brooklyn, what's wrong?"

"I fell. My head is bleeding. I'm in a lot of pain and can't move. It makes me sick." The words tumbled out of her mouth as panic set in.

"I'm sending an ambulance. I'll meet them there with the code to the garage. Hang on, Brooklyn. It's going to be okay," Giana told her.

"Okay, I'm getting sleepy. Wake me up when you get here," Brooklyn told her, setting the phone down on her chest. It was too heavy to hold on to.

"Brooklyn! Turn on your speaker. You can't go to sleep."

Gathering her strength, Brooklyn lifted the phone and squinted. It was hard to see. She pushed the screen where she hoped the right button was.

"…picking pizza flavors?" Pippa's voice sounded really loud.

"Pippa! Brooklyn hurt herself," Giana told her. "You and Aspen keep her talking as I drive. Don't let her go to sleep."

"Brooklyn! Open your eyes," Aspen ordered.

"You guys are bossy," Brooklyn whispered as she tried to block out the loud sound.

"Don't go to sleep!" Pippa demanded. "We'll tell your daddy you were naughty."

"So?" Brooklyn muttered with her eyes closed.

"Your eyes aren't supposed to be resting right now," Aspen told her. "I can tell you're not following directions. Your daddy will spank your bottom."

"Hard!" Pippa added.

"We'll get to watch," Aspen threatened.

Oh, no! She couldn't believe she was going to be spanked with an audience. Brooklyn wasn't a pretty crier. She got all snotty and blotchy. Forcing her eyes open halfway, she whispered, "Fine. I'm awake."

"Thank you, Brooklyn," Pippa told her. "Do you have Fluffikins?"

"No."

"Giana will remember him when you go in the ambulance," Aspen assured her.

"I can't go to the hospital," Brooklyn said. "I'll be okay in a few minutes."

"We're close, Brooklyn. You'll hear the garage door soon. It's me. You're safe," Giana told her.

"You're still on the line?" Brooklyn asked.

"Yes, I'm here," Giana assured her.

Struggling to pull herself together, Brooklyn needed to act. "Giana, I don't have insurance. I can't pay."

"I'm here, Brooklyn. That's the door you hear," Giana told her.

"Giana?" Brooklyn asked.

"Hey, Brooklyn. I'm here." Giana stepped around Brooklyn's form to kneel next to her inside the pantry. She brushed Brooklyn's hair from her face. "I brought some hot guys to help take care of you. Mark's a paramedic. He's good. Let him check you out."

"You're trying to distract me," Brooklyn said. Even with her hazy vision, she could see her friend's face etched with concern. "My head really hurts."

"You did a job on yourself, Brooklyn." Mark's voice was deep and calm. "We're going to get you fixed up. Can you tell me what happened?"

"I hit my head." Brooklyn hated the sound of her voice. Why did she sound so weak? She tried to roll over, but froze when she felt like she'd throw up. "Sick."

"Are you nauseous when you move?"

"It's bad."

"So, let's not do that right now. Lie still and let me see what's happening."

His voice quieted as he talked to someone behind him. "Give me a neck brace and find a towel or something to wipe some of this blood up."

"Did you fall off the chair?" Mark asked, turning back to her.

"Yes."

"That sucks. I'm sorry, Brooklyn. I'm going to put this around your neck to protect your spine in case you hurt it."

Giana held Brooklyn's head stable as Mark guided the neck brace into place.

"Do you have any idea when you fell?"

Brooklyn tried to think. She'd planned to search for something for dinner when she finished. "Four?"

"Did everything go black when you hit your head?"

"White. Then, black."

"Let's get a board and get Brooklyn out of here. She's hung out in the pantry too long," Giana suggested.

"Could I get a bandage? I don't know where they are," Brooklyn whispered, feeling tears roll down her cheeks. Her head hurt so badly. "An aspirin? I don't know where those are either?"

"We're going to get you something for the pain," Mark promised. "I bet you have a whopper of a headache."

"Worst ever."

"We're going to roll you over, Brooklyn. Don't try to help us. Just let us move you," Giana told her.

"No!" Brooklyn protested urgently. She gagged as her world whirled around her and her stomach lurched. In a few minutes, they had her secure on a stiff board. "Please don't move me," she begged.

"I'm sorry, Brooklyn. We need to take care of you and this protects your spine," Giana explained, brushing Brooklyn's hair from her eyes.

"Let's get her out to the bus," Mark said softly.

Brooklyn braced herself.

CHAPTER 15

All the movements blurred together until they set her on the stretcher. She blinked in the cool night air. When had the sun set? That question disappeared from her mind as they eased the stretcher down the stairs, jostling her. Brooklyn swallowed hard, trying not to throw up.

"I got you, Brooklyn," Giana assured her and held a bag near her mouth.

When they lifted her into the ambulance, Brooklyn lost control and retched. They tilted the board behind her to the side to keep her from choking. When she finished, they settled her back gently.

"You're okay, Brooklyn. We're going to get you put back together. I promise," Giana told her. "Big ouch now, as they start an IV. Do you want Fluffikins?"

"Ow! I wish Da… Caden was here," Brooklyn whispered, still with it enough not to blurt "Daddy."

"Caden would want to be here too. Fluffikins?" Giana checked on her earlier question.

"Let Fluffikins stay at home. I'm too messy. I want him

safe." Brooklyn closed her eyes. Giana was here now. Brooklyn wasn't alone. She could rest.

"Uh, uh, Brooklyn! Keep those eyes open. No sleeping for you," Mark demanded.

Sighing, she followed his directions. Maybe she could doze with her eyes open.

"Talk to me, Brooklyn. Tell me about your family," Giana interrupted her plan.

Between Mark and Giana, she didn't have a chance to snooze. That became even more impossible when they reached the emergency department. The flurry of activities overwhelmed her. She clung to Giana's hand as her lifeline between tests, injections, and stitches. Her headache never got better.

Completely exhausted and overwhelmed, Brooklyn sat on the edge of the bed, waiting for her discharge papers. She pulled at the stiff, blood-soaked neckline of her shirt, suspecting it would never be the same. All she wanted to do was take a shower and sleep forever.

They wouldn't send her home without someone to stay with her. Giana had to return to the firehouse to take care of the paperwork, so Aspen and Pippa had already packed a change of clothes and necessities. They should be there to pick her up by the time the hospital released her.

"Little girl…"

Her head popped up at the sound of his voice. Surely, she was imagining it. That quick motion made her weave with dizziness.

"Whoa, Brookie. Take it easy." Caden steadied her with his powerful hands on her shoulders.

She stared at him. His skin and uniform were dirty, and he smelled like he hadn't showered for days. She reached a hand up to grab his shirt. "You're here? I'm not imagining you?" Brooklyn asked, almost afraid to find out she was hallucinating. The material felt solid in her fist.

Caden leaned forward to kiss her lightly. "I'm here. I got home and found a lot of blood smeared on the floor. Are you okay?"

"I fell. My head split open. They had to shave part of my head," she told him as tears ran down her cheeks.

"I'm so sorry. Hair will regrow, sweetheart. Don't cry. That will make your head hurt," Caden said.

"It already throbs," she whined.

"Badly, I bet. Zale is talking to the doctor so he can tell me how to help you."

"The entire team is back?"

"Yes. Jerico is giving them my insurance information. I had you added to my account before I left," Caden told her.

"Really? I was so scared. I tried to talk them out of bringing me here, but they didn't listen."

"It's a good thing they didn't," Zale said, catching the end of her statement as he walked in the door.

Brooklyn was so glad to see him. Zale would take care of her. He lifted her chin to check out her eyes and winked. "You aren't supposed to have this much excitement when we're out of town. You scared us."

"I'm sorry," she said, tearing up.

"Don't cry, Brooklyn. Think happy thoughts. Your daddy is here," Zale reminded her.

Brooklyn blinked the moisture from her eyes and leaned on her daddy's chest. "I'm so glad you're here."

He looked at Caden and reported, "Sixteen stitches, probable concussion, no brain swelling or skull fracture. She's got nausea meds on board and can take acetaminophen when she gets home. I've got you covered on that to protect her stomach."

"Thanks, Zale. I don't know what we'd do without you," Caden told him.

"I don't plan on your ever finding that out. Now, they're going to send you home. Sponge bath tonight. Bath tomorrow. You can't get those stitches wet for a while."

"Can I take this off?" Brooklyn reached up carefully to touch the tight bandage around her head. "This is making my headache worse."

"Not for a while. It keeps you from bleeding. From what we saw in Caden's kitchen, you need every drop of blood left in you to stay there." Zale told her.

"I'll clean it up when I get home," she promised Caden. She definitely didn't want to mess up his immaculate house.

"You will not. It's Daddy's job," Caden told her.

"Okay! I've got your discharge papers. Now I understand why they call you a special forces team. I've never seen things move so fast. I think I need to find my own six buff guys," the fifty-something nurse told them with a twinkle in her eyes.

The woman in scrubs looked sternly at Caden, who cradled Brooklyn to his chest. "You take care of her. She is the sweetest patient we've had for a long time."

"Definitely. She's going to be wrapped in bubble wrap for a while," Caden assured her.

"Thank you for helping me," Brooklyn told her.

"I'm glad your soldier got back to take care of you. Let him."

Brooklyn watched the nurse disappear from the room as her kind words resonated inside her aching head. She relaxed completely against Caden's solid form. "You make everything better, Daddy."

He lifted her hand to his lips and kissed her softly. "Let's go home, little girl."

Jerico had pulled Caden's truck up to the entrance for him. He opened the door, and Caden lifted her inside. Her daddy buckled her seatbelt before closing the door as softly as possible. She propped her elbow on the console and cradled the side of her skull in her hand. It hurt too badly to rest her head on the seat. Through the window, Brooklyn could hear the men talking.

"That head is going to hurt. I'll bring over some painkillers and nausea medicine. An icepack is a good idea. Do you have a bag of frozen peas?" Zale asked.

"You made that a staple in our freezers," Caden said. "Let her sleep or wake her up?"

"Clean her up and put her to bed with some meds. It's important to check on her for the first four hours. More than that time has passed since she fell. You're going to have a light-sleep night tonight. Do you need the team to take turns monitoring her so you can rest?"

"My little girl. I'll take care of her. We'll recover together," Caden told him.

"I'll lobby for several days off for you to recover. We'll get at least three. If you need more…"

"I'll take personal time," Caden said brusquely.

"Noted. Keep me in the loop. We'll let Hank lead training for a while. I get the impression he'll have something unique up his sleeve," Jerico said.

"Take her home. I'll drop off some meds at the front door soon," Zale said, hurrying back to his vehicle.

In seconds, the driver's door opened, and Caden heaved himself into the truck. She could tell he was operating on his very last bit of energy and regretted adding to his exhaustion. He should be in bed sleeping. The entire team should have celebrated their return with their little girls.

"I'm sorry. I'm so stupid and clumsy," she whispered, overwhelmed by how much trouble she had caused.

Caden turned to her immediately and ran a hand over her

cheek. "You aren't stupid, little girl. Accidents happen. You didn't plan this."

"You could drop me off at a hotel," she suggested. Her life was so screwed up. Maybe some people were unlucky at life. She definitely was.

"That's never going to happen," he told her sternly. "I will never abandon you. I'm your daddy, and I love you."

"But I'm so much trouble," she said sadly. "I won't think badly of you if you decide I cause too much havoc." Her tears exhausted, Brooklyn couldn't even cry.

"If you didn't have a head injury, I'd spank your bottom now. Given your condition, I'm going to wait to punish you for talking so badly about yourself," he told her in a hard voice that she didn't dare argue with.

"Sorry," she squeaked.

"No more talk about leaving or being a bother or I'll add additional punishment to my list."

"Yes, sir."

"Yes, Daddy," he corrected.

"Yes, Daddy."

"I missed you, little girl. Spending time in the hospital when I return from a mission outshines arriving home to an empty house. One makes my heart hurt from worry, the other rips my heart out of my chest. Which do you think I prefer?"

"My being in the emergency department." The band around her chest loosened as she realized he really meant it.

"Exactly. Now, are you ready to go home?"

"Yes, Daddy."

CHAPTER 16

The rattle of the heavy door woke Brooklyn as her daddy pulled into the garage. She jerked and groaned when she jostled her head. Pressing a hand to her temple under the heavy bandaging, Brooklyn waited for her brain to stop sloshing around inside her skull.

"Let's get you inside, sweetheart."

When he opened her door, she gathered the last of her energy to move. Caden scooped her gently from her seat and carried her into the house. Walking through the rooms, he took her directly to the bathroom and stood her next to the bathtub. Caden turned on the water to warm before saying, "Let's get you cleaned up."

Brooklyn reached for the bottom of her T-shirt, but her daddy pulled her hands away. Grateful to have him take over, she stood there using her energy to remain upright. The pain in her head overwhelmed her thinking. Thank goodness her daddy was there to help her, and she'd let Giana take her to the hospital.

"Okay, baby girl. I'm going to sit you in the bathtub so we

can get you cleaned up for bed. No splashing. We can't get your bandages wet."

He lifted her into his arms and placed her bottom on a soft towel he'd placed in the bathtub. Supporting her with one hand, he used the plastic cup from the sink to pour water over her. Each cascade soothed her jangled nerves and relaxed her tense muscles. She melted as he spread the silky body wash over her skin.

By the time he'd rinsed the suds off, Brooklyn wasn't sure if she was awake or asleep. She roused when Caden stretched her out on the changing table in her nursery. "Cold," she whimpered at the feel of the waterproof material underneath her.

"Sorry, Brookie. I'll have you in bed soon."

He dragged the thick belt she'd noticed before across her tummy and snapped it into place. She shivered until he draped the soft blanket from her crib over her nude body. A kiss landed on her cheek.

"Stay still, little girl. Zale dropped off some medicine for you. Let's see if it will erase your headache, okay?"

"Please." What a relief it would be to stop this pounding.

Blinking awake as he turned her over on her side, Brooklyn automatically struggled.

"Stop, little girl. I'm going to give you some medicine to help your head."

"I'll need to sit up to swallow," she muttered.

"Little girls with hurt noggins don't take pills with their mouths," he told her. "Zale made you medicine that won't upset your stomach."

"He's so nice," Brooklyn said, melting onto the padding below her. Caden bent her legs and wrapped something behind her knees to hold them in place.

"Wait! What?" she protested as he separated her buttocks

and pressed a glob of something cold on the small ring of muscles hidden there.

"Relax, little girl. This is much better than a shot."

That made her stop for a second. His finger pressing into her bottom made her struggle to straighten her legs. Her energy evaporated quickly, and she panted, sagging in exhaustion.

"Trust Daddy to take care of you," he said quietly. "You want to feel better, don't you?"

"Yes," she whispered.

"Good girl."

Closing her eyes, she allowed him to press a thick item into her bottom, stretching that ring of muscles despite her attempts to stop him. The second slid inside easier. She shivered at the cold sensation filling her tight passage.

"I'll wrap you in a blanket in a few minutes, little girl. The medicine will warm up quickly as it melts. Let's get a diaper to protect you."

She held her breath, wondering if he would notice she'd used one of the diapers underneath. When Caden didn't say anything about it but simply released her knees and rolled her to her back, Brooklyn breathed a sigh of relief. The crinkly garment around her body lured her further into Little space. She didn't question the pacifier he brushed over her lips but welcomed it eagerly. A short time later, she cuddled onto her pillow on her side to avoid the wound on the back of her head and tumbled into sleep.

* * *

WAKING up in the morning light, Brooklyn found herself held against her daddy's bare chest. Her heart seemed to swell inside her chest as she processed he was home. She inhaled deeply, loving his scent—all warm and masculine.

The corners of her mouth tilted upward as she realized he must have showered after tucking her in bed.

His chest rose under her cheek with his deep and easy breath. She loved that he slept so well. She'd only seen Zale, Jerico, and Caden up close. The other guys had hung back away from their vehicle as Caden had carried her to the truck. Aspen, Pippa, and Giana had waited to make sure she was okay.

Brooklyn couldn't believe how they'd rallied around her. She'd missed having friends. On the run from Brent, Brooklyn had built up her defenses so high that she didn't trust anyone. Caden had shared these wonderful people with her.

She adjusted her head. That was enough to bring her pain to the forefront of her mind. Would her headache ever stop?

Her face heated remembering waking up so uncomfortable in the middle of the night after rolling onto her back, so the wound pressed hard on the pillow. Her gasp of pain had woken her daddy. Immediately alert, Caden had pressed another of the thick medicine suppositories into her bottom. Trapped between sleepiness and pain, she hadn't protested his intimate care as much. When he'd slipped between the sheets once again, he'd pulled her close and wrapped his arm around her to keep her off the stitches.

I should get up and let him sleep.

I don't want to move.

I'll move later.

"Are you hurting, Brookie?"

His sleep-roughened voice made her jump. That abrupt motion made her groan. Without hesitating, Caden rolled out of bed and scooped her gently up into his arms. "Hey, sweetheart. It's time for more medicine."

Even his slow pace affected Brooklyn, making her close

her eyes to hide. He kissed her forehead softly. "Daddy will make it better."

She kept her eyelids sealed shut as he set her on the changing table, unfastened the tape around her waist, and rolled Brooklyn to her side. Her daddy wiped the cold cloth over her skin, making her shiver both in response to the temperature and in fascination with Caden taking such intimate care of her.

"Sorry," she whispered.

"I've dreamed of having a very young little girl for as long as I can remember. Some daddies prefer sweet or bratty Middles or older Littles. I appreciate them too, but brave Littles who admit they love total care are superstars to me," he shared as he cleaned her skin thoroughly.

He guided a fresh wipe between her buttocks, paying special attention to the small entrance hidden there. She tried not to respond as the caresses on that nerve-rich area distracted Brooklyn from the lingering headache that plagued her. A moan slipped from her lips before she could stop it as her juices welled in response to his touch. Maybe he wouldn't notice.

"I know, little girl. Your bottom is very sensitive. After I get you cleaned up, Daddy's going to take your temperature before he gives you more medicine. I want to make sure you didn't catch anything at the hospital."

At the sound of a soft swoosh, she guessed he'd pulled a new wipe from the pack. Bracing herself for the cold sensation, Brooklyn wasn't prepared for him to shift her top knee forward to expose her pussy. He couldn't miss seeing how much she enjoyed his touch.

"I think my little girl enjoys her daddy's touch as much as I love taking care of her," Caden told her softly. His low voice made his comments so intimate and special as he rubbed over her sensitive clit, pushing her arousal higher. "Thank you for being Daddy's special girl. Let's get you feeling better so I can show you how much I love you."

"No!" she protested when his touch ended.

"Soon, Brookie. Now, Daddy needs to check your temperature."

She heard a click of the lubricant already placed for handy usage on the table and held her breath. The drawer opened underneath the padded top, and she could imagine what he saw. Several rustles later, the drawer closed.

"Did you explore Daddy's tools while I was gone, little girl?"

Oh, no! She'd tried to put everything back in place. "I got a pacifier out," Brooklyn confessed. He already knew about that.

"I'm glad you found something you enjoyed, little girl. From now on, this drawer is off limits. I'll set up a basket with fun things for you, like toys and pacifiers. That will be Brooklyn's stash, okay?"

"Okay, Daddy. I'll be good."

"Of course you will," he reassured her.

Caden applied a cold dollop of lubricant to her bottom's entrance. Brooklyn guessed this previously taboo spot would receive a lot of attention from her daddy. She squeezed that ring of muscles automatically trying to keep him out. His finger slid easily inside. *He's in control.*

"Relax, Brookie."

"I'm trying," she whispered.

"Daddy will help you practice. I'll touch you here often until you get used to it."

An image of stretching out bare bottomed over his thighs as they sat on the couch popped into her mind. His hand caressed her buttocks as he pressed a finger or two into her tight channel, distracting her completely from the movie playing on his TV. Perhaps he would put a jar of lubricant on the end table out where everyone would see it. The other Littles would guess immediately why the jar was there.

"Daddy, no."

"Don't tell Daddy no, little girl. That gets you a red bottom."

Immediately, the picture in her mind changed. Brooklyn imagined the sting and heat on her tender skin as he tended to her after reminding his little girl who was in charge.

"Want to tell Daddy what you're thinking about?" he asked as he spread the lubricant inside her tight channel.

"No," she whispered.

"Okay, sweetheart. You can have secret fantasies. I hope someday I'll make them come true."

He withdrew his finger and replaced it with the thick thermometer she'd discovered. He guided it deep into her before twisting and adjusting the device deeper inside Brooklyn. Finally, he cupped his hand over her bottom, holding it in place.

"Breathe, little girl."

She exhaled a long, shaky stream of air. Her attention focused on the cold intruder inside her bottom. *Little girls have their temperatures taken in their bottoms* repeated in her brain. Brooklyn slipped into a quiet place where she didn't have to worry about anything. The throbbing in her brain lessened slightly as she melted onto the table.

"That's my good girl. Here, sweetheart." Caden rubbed a smooth object across her lips and Brooklyn opened her mouth to accept it without peeking. The pacifier's large bulb filled her mouth, underlining her total submission.

Several long minutes later, he removed the thermometer from her bottom, leaving her empty. Caden quickly remedied that, inserting medicine deep into her bottom. His finger remained inside her until it no longer felt cold.

When he pulled another wipe from the box, she expected

him to clean up the lubricant that coated her. When that didn't happen, she peeked through her lashes to see him cleaning his fingers.

"What a good girl you are. I think that deserves a treat. Can you hold still for Daddy and keep your head steady?"

"Yes," she whispered.

He turned her over on the changing table and pressed her knees apart. "No wiggles, little girl."

Caden drew a line with one finger across her inner thigh to trail through her pussy. He traced her drenched entrance, brushing over her clit. His hand pressed her thigh down to the table when she lifted her hips. A thrill coursed through her as he controlled her movements.

"Uh, uh, little girl."

Wide-eyed, Brooklyn watched him rub and caress her, hitting sensitive, thrilling spots she didn't know existed. Her daddy understood her pleasure better than she did. She devoured his chiseled nude body as he loomed over her.

The hunger on his face elevated her already sky-high desire. Caden's hand wrapped around his shaft, pulling it roughly from base to tip. She could see small droplets glistening on the head of his cock. He quickly pushed both of them to a stunning climax and marked her with his essence.

"Mine, little girl. You're mine."

CHAPTER 17

Caden kissed the top of his little girl's head. Brooklyn had chosen a favorite spot to rest and watch movies as she recuperated. Cuddled up next to him on the large couch, she sat as close as possible on the same cushion. He loved having her close.

"I need to go change the laundry, Brookie."

"You can't go right now. It's the most exciting part!"

He'd discovered the key to keeping her quiet and entertained. It didn't take a detective to deduce her favorite video. They'd already seen this one three times. One glance at her eager face and he couldn't go anywhere.

"Thank you for reminding me, little girl."

Caden relaxed on the soft leather couch and enjoyed the rest of the show. Spending time with his little girl was much more important than laundry. When it was over, he asked, "Shall I play it one more time?"

She shook her head hesitantly. It had taken a couple of days for her dizziness to abate. He hated to see her expecting negative effects when she moved. If only he'd been here.

"Stop, Daddy. You've got that look again. You had nothing

to do with my clumsiness. Like you've told me a million times, it's called an accident for a reason. It's not an on purpose."

"Okay, sweetheart. I'll try to remember that. Zale thought you were healing incredibly well."

"Thank goodness he took off that awful bandage. My head is much better now," she told him. "If I could only wash my hair…"

"We'll try that dry shampoo tomorrow. Give your skin time to heal."

"But my head is itchy now."

Caden had already wiped the blood caking her hair with a damp cloth. That had done nothing for her itchy scalp. "Come sit on a stool at the island and let Daddy check your stitches. Maybe it wouldn't make a difference if I played hairdresser today."

"Yes! Thank you, Daddy."

She quickly maneuvered away from him to stand up. Caden groaned and got up from his comfy spot. He'd been at home for two days with his Little. Caden wasn't used to sitting around. If Brooklyn kept making progress, he'd at least go for a run tomorrow.

Halfway to the kitchen, his phone rang. His heart froze seeing Jerico's name. "Don't tell me."

"Okay. I won't. We're not deployed. I have a little girl over here who's making herself sick worrying about Brooklyn. Is there any way Aspen could come over for a short visit?"

Caden studied Brooklyn. Her color had improved. She'd taken a long nap in her nursery after lunch. "Would you like a visitor? Aspen is worried about you."

"I'd love to see Aspen. Could Giana and Pippa come over too? They never got to see my dollhouse."

When she bounced with excitement, Caden wrapped a

hand over her shoulder and stopped her motion. "You'll have to stay calm. No jostling your brain."

"I'll be so still you'll wonder if I'm a tree!"

Caden looked at her skeptically but spoke into the phone. "Come over in an hour. I need to get Brooklyn ready for company."

"You got it. Want me to call Koa and Zale?" Jerico asked.

"Yes." Caden added, "Better call Hank and Max. They'd probably like to visit as well. Stress that it's a quick visit this first time."

"You got it. Short visit. Notify the team." Jerico disconnected the call with that crisp, short, military-style review of the essential message to share with everyone.

"They're going to bring dinner," he told Brooklyn.

"I didn't hear you say anything about food."

"I know those guys. They'll want to help. Food is important to soldiers. They'll descend on us with enough stuff to feed an army." Caden smiled to himself. He'd worked with a lot of teams during his time in the military. Whoever had put this group together had outdone themselves.

"They've all been so nice to me," Brooklyn said softly as Caden picked her up and sat her on a stool.

"I'd hope so," Caden told her before stepping into the laundry room to grab a clean towel from the stack on the dryer. He'd given up putting everything in the cabinet as he folded it. Brooklyn had needed him to hold her. As much as Caden had pushed the memory from his mind, walking into see a blood-soaked towel with more evidence of a serious accident or attack smeared on the tile floor had scared him—more than some of the horrendous events he'd witnessed in the military.

"I'm okay, Daddy," she whispered to reassure him.

"You see too much, little girl." Caden had always prided

himself on his poker face. Brooklyn could read him like a book.

"I'm supposed to, Daddy. I love you."

"Thank goodness. Now, no squirming. Let me see your stitches."

Caden carefully drew a few rogue strands of hair that had gotten tousled out of place away from the wound. The skin was pink and not as angry as it had been before. "Your wound looks good. I'm game to try my hand at dry shampoo if you'd like."

"Oh, yes! Thank you!"

Caden read the directions carefully as she fidgeted. Wanting to be extra careful, he noted the warnings.

"Daddy. It's not that hard. Sprinkle it on and brush it through. I could do it," she offered.

"No way, little girl." He sent her a steely glance that squelched her wiggles. Caden shook the container and applied the powder at the ends of her tresses as far as possible from the wound. Some of the material blew toward her stitches, making him second-guess whether this was smart.

"What's wrong?" she asked impatiently.

"The powder is floating all over."

They looked at each other for a moment. He could see the disappointment in her eyes. Could he use something as a barricade for the powder? What could he lay over the stitches that wouldn't wet or stick to them and would be easily removed?

"I've got an idea."

He could feel her eyes on him as he opened the drawer where he kept his potholders. He picked up a silicone square he used as a hot pad to protect the table from casserole dishes. Caden grabbed sharp shears and cut a piece slightly larger than her injury. He washed and dried it carefully.

"Okay, sweetheart. You're going to have to stay still so you don't knock this off," he told her and had to steel himself from smiling as she stiffened into the perfect soldier on alert posture.

"I won't move," she promised.

Placing the strip carefully, he picked up the shaker bottle and applied more to her head. "This is working, little girl. Keep that statue thing going."

Soon, he brushed her hair thoroughly, leaving a sprinkle of rusty flakes on her shoulders and the floor. The tension in her shoulders eased. "Feel better, Brookie?"

"I can't wait to wash my hair for real, but this is heaven. You're really good at this."

"Want Daddy to braid your hair to keep it out of the way?"

"Yes, please."

He quickly removed the silicon barrier and finished her hair, giving her the first braid to hold while he did the second. "Okay, sweetheart. Hold the ends of this one, and I'll go get something to tie around them."

He was back in a flash with the cotton string he used to tie meat together for smoking. Cutting a couple of pieces, he fashioned small, adorable bows on the end of each braid. "How's that?"

"Thank you. You're good at this."

"Braiding?" he asked with a smile.

"Being my daddy."

His heart skipped a beat. For years he'd waited to find the perfect Little who matched his style of care. He'd found her. Stepping forward, he hugged Brooklyn tight and picked her up in his arms to settle her on his hip. She rested her head on his shoulder as he swayed back and forth.

Caden could see her eyelids fluttering shut. The flurry of

activity had worn her out. He carried Brooklyn to her nursery and tucked his exhausted Little under the soft comforter. "Go to sleep, baby."

"My friends are coming over," she protested, yawning.

"They'll be glad to let you nap for an hour. Then you can play." He tucked Fluffikins into her arms and smiled as she rubbed her nose in the bunny's soft fur. When she had settled, he pressed her pacifier into her mouth and rubbed her back until she relaxed and tumbled into sleep.

A quick text to the group chat delayed everyone's arrival for a couple of hours. The answers popped in immediately. The team would be glad to come when Brooklyn was ready to see them. Her health was most important.

Caden forced himself from the nursery door. He could listen in on the monitor app to hear when she woke up. Carrying his phone with him, Caden headed for the kitchen to make the macaroni and cheese concoction that all the Littles loved. It would be hot and bubbly when she woke up.

* * *

Sniffing, Brooklyn blinked away her sleepiness. She rolled onto her back without thinking and yelped. Turning back on her side, she covered her stitches automatically, protecting them a bit too late.

Caden ran in seconds later. Literally raced to her side. Zale arrived right behind him. "Brookie, what's wrong?"

"I'm okay. I'm so stupid and laid on my stitches," she said.

"Sleepy, not stupid," Caden corrected before helping her sit up and turn slightly so he and Zale could check her head. "The good news is you didn't rip any stitches. You're fine."

Zale seconded that assessment. "I'm glad everything's okay, but I bet that hurt."

She nodded, trying to be brave. "I don't want any pain medicine. That makes me too sleepy." She looked toward the door and saw the entire group clustered at the entrance to her nursery.

"How about if your daddy gets you some juice to wake up, and we put some ice on your head to see if that helps?" Zale suggested.

"Okay." She swallowed hard and immediately was thirsty. How did Zale know what she needed before she did?

"Come here, Brookie." Caden carefully lifted her from her crib, supporting her head as he learned to do since her injury. "She's okay. Just a bit of a headache. Darn stitches."

Brooklyn looked at everyone and whispered, "Hi!"

The crowd led her back to the kitchen, where Zale grabbed a bag of frozen peas from the freezer. After handing it to Caden, he made himself at home, getting a sippy cup of juice for her while Caden sat down at the table with Brooklyn on his lap.

"Come join us," he invited the Littles.

Immediately, they swarmed the table. Talking in quiet whispers, they chose their seats. Soon the women had something to drink in front of them.

The cold pack on her head helped almost instantly. After a big drink of the tropical fruit juice, Brooklyn rallied. "Hi, girls. Thank you for helping me."

"Of course. While the guys are out of town, we always support each other. You don't have to thank us. Maybe I'll need someone to bail me out during the next deployment," Aspen said.

"Bail you out? Like from jail?" Brooklyn asked in confusion.

"Little girl. What do you have planned?" Zale growled.

"No. Not jail, Daddy. I mean, if my car breaks down or I

get sad, I'd need you all to come to my rescue," Aspen said quickly.

"Better," Zale told her.

"I've never been so glad to see anyone, Giana," Brooklyn spoke up, distracting everyone from their focus on Aspen.

Her new friend mouthed, *I owed you one.*

"I was glad to see you when you popped that door open and whisked me away from Tom," Giana said with a shiver. "I'm glad I was on call so I could come ride with you to the hospital. Let's call it even now."

"I like that idea," Brooklyn said. She lifted her nose to sniff. "It smells really good in here."

"Are you hungry, Brookie?" Caden asked.

"Five more minutes with the icepack on, little girl," Zale announced. "That's enough time for the team to get the food together, and your daddies will bring each of you a plate."

Brooklyn looked at Caden and whispered, "I have to potty."

"Let's go get that taken care of now. Guys, I'll be right back," Caden said to the other men as he carried her to the large master bathroom.

When they were alone, Caden instructed, "You hold on to the peas, and I'll get your pants."

In a short time, Brooklyn sat on the toilet. Caden hadn't let her out of his sight since her accident. He always stayed with her in the bathroom now. It was getting easier to relax and pee. Inside, even though she was embarrassed, Brooklyn loved having him there. Nothing was off limits to Caden.

At least he hadn't dressed her in a diaper today. Brooklyn blushed remembering how she'd actually used one a couple of times while groggy with the medicine. Caden hadn't minded cleaning her up at all. She smiled a bit, remembering how much he'd seemed to enjoy taking care of her.

"What are you thinking, little girl? You're not plotting fun with your friends, are you?" Caden asked, looking at her suspiciously.

"No, Daddy. I'm happy being little here with you."

"I love you, Brookie."

"I love you, Daddy."

CHAPTER 18

A couple of days later, Caden's refrigerator still groaned with the leftovers of the food their friends had brought over for the gathering. Brooklyn checked out each of the yummy dishes inside and tried to decide what she wanted to eat. Popping open the container of wings Koa had brought, Brooklyn chose one to munch on as she decided what else sounded good. Everyone had laughed as Koa had pulled the foil off his dish, except for Giana, who'd rolled her eyes so hard they almost made a noise.

"Do not encourage him or you'll be eating wings for the next ten years," Giana had warned.

Brooklyn didn't really understand why it was so funny, but figured there was a backstory she'd missed out on. The team worked and played so closely together they had a lot of history together. All she knew was that Koa's wings were yummy.

Grabbing a few cold boiled shrimp and some cocktail sauce, Brooklyn rounded out her feast with some cut-up apples and caramel dip. She carried everything carefully over to the table before grabbing one of the sippy cups Caden had already filled for her in the refrigerator. She took a small testing sip and grinned. Chocolate milk. Finding the treat on her first try was amazing.

She'd just sat down to eat when her phone buzzed. Giana's name flashed on the screen. "Hi!" Brooklyn said after accepting the call.

"Hi! Whatcha doing?"

"I'm eating lunch. How about you?"

"I finished about fifteen minutes ago. Want me to call you back later?" Giana asked.

"As long as you don't mind if I'm chewing, I'd love to have company."

"I hoped you might like even more company."

"You're coming over to play?" Brooklyn asked as she wiggled with excitement.

"If you're interested, I'll come over to pick you up. I wanted to go get coffee, but Daddy doesn't like me to go to the coffee shop alone." She lowered her voice to match Koa's growly tone and said, "Those guys are just hanging out there to pick up women."

"That's hilarious. You sound like him," Brooklyn said and giggled.

"I have a two-for-one coupon, Brooklyn, so I can treat you to some java. Take pity on me. I have a bunch of reports to work on, and I need the caffeine."

"I don't know, Giana. I don't think I should go anywhere. Brent could be out there somewhere. It would be my luck to run into him at the coffee shop." Brooklyn wrung her hands, automatically scared by the thought of being out in public.

"How long has it been since you saw him? Surely, he's moved on."

Giana's words made her stop and think for a minute. But after hiding for so long, she couldn't imagine that he'd suddenly decide to stop pursuing her. Brooklyn shook her head to remind herself that she never took risks, and still he found her repeatedly. "Brent has followed me for a couple of years now, Giana. I don't think he'll give up now."

"That jerk saw Caden in action. He had to notice that your car was packed. Won't he think you left town while he was in jail?" Giana asked.

When Brooklyn stayed quiet, Giana quickly apologized. "I'm sorry, Brooklyn. I'm pressuring you to do something you don't want to do. My coffee addiction is not that important. I hate to see a jerk win and for you to lose the fun in your life. Tom scared me, just like Brent frightens you. You should have Caden teach you some self-defense moves. Then you could take your power back."

That last statement repeated in Brooklyn's mind. *Take your power back.* Giana was right. For too long Brent had threatened and harassed her. Who gave up everything in their life to follow someone out of spite? Maybe it was possible to live without fear. Swallowing hard, she decided.

"Is there a coffee shop far from our old apartment complex?" Brooklyn asked. "It was on the east side of town."

"Of course. There's one about five blocks from Caden's house. A small independent shop. I like those better than the big chains. Are you thinking we could zip in and out?" Giana asked with a hopeful tone.

"Yes, but Caden and Zale say no driving until next week."

"I'll come get you. That's better anyway. We'll be together."

Brooklyn exhaled with relief. She'd feel better with Giana. "Okay. Let's do it."

"I'll be at your door in ten minutes."

Brooklyn ran into the bedroom and raided Caden's closet. Grabbing an oversized sweatshirt and a hat, Brooklyn tried to camouflage herself as much as possible. Daring was one thing, reckless was another. She'd secured her hair in a ponytail and hid it under the baseball cap after pulling on the bulky top.

She looked at her phone for a few seconds as she debated whether to tell her daddy. He'd worry, and she'd distracted him enough. Her head ached slightly as her thoughts whirled around in her brain. Brooklyn took several deep breaths to relax, and the pain decreased.

A car horn tooted in her driveway, speeding her out the door. Brooklyn didn't have a key. She hadn't ever needed to leave alone. An image flashed into her brain of a single key hanging next to the garage. She darted to the keyholder, borrowed it, and secured the front door behind her.

"Caffeine, here we come!" Giana greeted her cheerfully. "Before we go, are you sure you're ready for this? We don't have to go. I could come in, and we could splurge on chocolate milk."

"Can we return if I get scared?"

"Immediately. Tell me and we're out of there," Giana reassured her.

Several minutes later, Brooklyn sat focused on the door as she sipped on a sinfully sweet, caffeinated beverage with whipped cream on top. She moaned with delight at the delicious taste. "This is heaven."

"You're telling me. I think I was going through withdrawals," Giana said with a laugh.

"Wait until I tell you about the call we got yesterday." She launched into a long story about a cat stuck up in a tree and a random dog walker who'd allowed the four dogs he was exercising to wrap around the fireman's ladder. Of course, they'd yanked the bottom of the ladder out, making the would-be rescuer grab onto the tree to keep from tumbling. The visual image of the fireman left dangling from the limb while the cat nimbly walked over his hands to shimmy back down the trunk had Brooklyn almost rolling from her chair.

"I'm glad your job has some entertaining times as well," Brooklyn told her. "I'm sure it's stressful."

"It is. We see people on their worst days. Not just for fires, but for many medical emergencies as well."

"Mark did an amazing job, taking care of me. You have to be a special kind of person to reassure people in trouble. Would it be weird if I wrote him a thank-you letter?" Brooklyn asked.

"Not at all. Most of us have a file of special notes we've received over the years. Remembering how I made a difference for someone always makes me work harder at the drills to stay in top shape."

"I bet. I'll do it and bring it to the next gathering if you'd take it to Mark."

"Of course. You'll make his day. Like you made mine by coming out with me. How are you doing?"

"I've enjoyed this." Brooklyn sucked the last of her iced coffee up the straw. She glanced around the coffee shop, making sure no one was paying any attention to them. She'd had fun with Giana, but now wanted to retreat to the safety of Caden's house.

"Ready to go?" Giana guessed before Brooklyn could ask.

"If you don't mind."

"Of course not. Let's go."

In minutes, Brooklyn let herself back into Caden's house. She leaned against the door and stared around the interior. It seemed different somehow. Like the space had changed from a sanctuary to a home. Hugging her arms around her waist, Brooklyn celebrated. The threat of Brent hadn't ruled her life today.

After returning the key, she skipped down the hallway to return Caden's things. He'd be home in an hour or so. Brooklyn retrieved Fluffikins from the couch where she'd left him and went to her nursery to play.

Brooklyn had finished putting together the border of a gigantic puzzle when she heard the garage door open. She smiled at her daddy as he walked into the nursery. "Hi!"

"You had a good day today," he guessed, setting a heavy sack on the table before kneeling by her side to kiss her.

She stiffened when he pulled back to look at her. She'd forgotten to brush her teeth. "Can you taste the chocolate milk I drank?" she lied.

His gaze narrowed further, making her feel like a pinned butterfly in front of a scientist. "No, but I can taste the coffee. Where did you get coffee?"

Crap! What could she say? Some truth was better than none. "Giana came over and brought a treat."

"Oh, so I'll find two cups in the trash?"

Crap, crap, crap! She hadn't thought of that. *Think fast, Brooklyn!* "No… She took them with her, because… Because they recycle at her house. Giana is very dedicated to the environment."

Her already panicked heart rate exploded when Caden reached into his back pocket and pulled out his phone. Seconds later, he said, "Koa. Do you recycle?"

Caden kept his gaze focused on her and acknowledged Koa's response, "Thank you. I'll explain tomorrow."

"Want to try a different story?" he asked as he watched her squirm.

Her mind went blank. Caught, she couldn't think of anything else to say but, "Sorry."

"Tell me the truth."

"Giana wanted to go for coffee. Koa won't let her go alone because people flirt with her at the coffee shop."

"Including himself," Caden agreed. "Keep going. Giana wanted to get coffee."

"She convinced me to go with her. I was scared to go, but Brent hasn't been around for so long, and I wanted to have fun with Giana. Brent robbed me of so much." She held her breath, hoping he would understand.

"He has," Caden agreed. "Did anything concerning happen? Did you see Brent or his car?"

"No, nothing happened. We had a blast. It was incredible to live normally. Giana chose a small coffee shop close to here, so we'd be far from our old apartments where Brent saw me last."

"Smart. Anything else you need to tell me?" Caden asked.

"No, that's all. I borrowed the key by the garage door and locked the house. I tried to do everything the right way," she said, hoping to convince him. Caden had seemed to understand her actions so far. Why did Brooklyn have a hunch she was still in trouble?

"You did everything right except for two things. You didn't call me to tell me you were leaving and you lied to me."

"Oh, I didn't want to disturb you. What if you were busy?"

"We leave our phones in lockers, little girl, while we're out on maneuvers and can't be interrupted. You should leave a message if I don't pick up."

His steady gaze seemed to see into her soul. Her headache returned as her stress level rose. Lifting her hand to her forehead, Brooklyn caved.

"You're right. I should have called. And…" she hesitated a second before admitting, "I'm sorry I lied about going out."

"What do you think I would have done?" he asked quietly.

"Forbid me?"

"I'll admit that would have been my first impulse. I hope I would have listened to your point about having already let Brent ruin so much for you." Caden shook his head slowly as if he blamed himself.

"It's not your fault that I lied," she whispered as her stomach churned with worry. She rubbed her belly absentmindedly. She'd messed this up so badly.

"No. That was your decision. I think you know instinctively that lying is bad."

"Yes, Daddy," she whispered. "Are you going to spank me?"

"Yes. This makes two on your discipline list. But I won't punish you until your concussion improves. When you can think clearly, we'll write some rules for us both."

Did she hear that right? "Daddies have rules too?"

"Definitely. We'll discuss all our guidelines when your brain has healed. Now, I think you need some headache medicine."

She nodded. "My head hurts. And it's all my fault. When I get upset, the ache comes back."

"It will take you some time to heal, little girl." Caden rose and scooped Brooklyn into his arms. He walked over to the changing table and set her feet on the carpet. Carefully, he drew her T-shirt over her head and stripped off the rest of her clothing. When she was nude, he boosted her onto the changing table and strapped her into position on her side.

His hand rubbed over her bottom as he told her, "Zale sent home some new medicine for you. This is a liquid. It will help your tummy work better as well."

"My tummy?" she echoed as Caden moved from her side to grab that bulging sack from the table.

He set it behind her, out of her sight. Caden opened the lubricant and prepared her bottom as normal, spreading the slippery mixture over her sensitive bottom hole and pressing two fingers inside to coat the walls of her tight channel. When he withdrew his touch, she slumped in relief on the table.

The crinkle of a package opening made her tense once again. Caden held her firmly in place as he pressed the rounded head of something to her small entrance. Brooklyn gasped as a cold device stretched her tight ring of muscles. "What's that, Daddy? It's too big."

"You can take it easily, Brookie. Relax. Tightening up won't keep this out. You'll only make your headache worse. Take a deep breath with Daddy." He waited for her to follow his instructions. "Now exhale all that air."

As he blew out audibly with her, Caden pressed the object into her bottom. The thick device filled her narrow opening, commanding her attention. "Good girl. Now the headache medicine."

Over her hip, she could see him fill a thick plastic tube. He drew liquid up into it like a huge syringe with black slashes on the side showing the dosage. When he reached a red line, Caden moved the dose behind her. The device inside her jostled before the medicine gushed into her bottom.

"No, Daddy!" she protested and tried to wiggle, but Caden held her in place with a hand on her hip.

"Don't be bad, little girl. It's not hurting you. I'll slow down the flow a bit. You've taken about half the medicine. Zale told me your headache should fade quickly."

By the time the insert in her bottom stopped jostling, a haze had fallen over her. The strange sensation of having her bottom filled vanished from her thoughts as a peaceful calm captured her attention. She closed her eyes, basking in the pleasurable sensation. Her headache wasn't even a memory.

"This is nice, Daddy."

"Good, sweetheart. Daddy's going to help you come so your climax squeezes the medicine deep into your bottom." He shifted her to lie on her back with her knees widely spread. "Such a beautiful little girl. Let's see how many times you can come for me."

"Okay." That sounded good. Why would she ever turn pleasure down? A buzzing sound registered on the edges of her attention. Brooklyn didn't pay attention to it until he trailed it through the pink folds of her pussy. She opened her eyes to see Caden caress her with a pink wand vibrator.

The view pushed her arousal even higher. It seemed so decadent to be displayed in front of him while he played on her body's reactions. Already wet from him giving her medicine and the plug in her bottom, Brooklyn's slick juices gushed from her, coating her skin as Caden teased her. When he tapped it on her clitoris, Brooklyn heard herself moan. The intermittent vibration made her lift her hips, following the stimulation when he lifted the device.

Caden relented and held the stimulator in place. Instantly, her muscles contracted, and her climax exploded, shaking her with its intensity. Before she could recover, he rekindled the thrilling sensations. When she couldn't take any more, her daddy turned off the vibrator and soothed her with soft strokes on her skin. As she drifted off to sleep, Caden wiped away her slick juices and wrapped a diaper around her hips.

CHAPTER 19

"Hi, Zale. Thanks for calling to check on Brooklyn. She hasn't needed any medicine for a week now."

Brooklyn colored furiously as she eavesdropped on her daddy's conversation. As happy as she was to be headache free, she was a bit sad she wouldn't need the extra-close care Caden had lavished on her. She'd loved being super little for him. The medicine had erased her self-consciousness and allowed her to bask in his intimate attention.

After a slight pause, Caden continued, "I agree. She's definitely on the path to feeling one hundred percent. Can I ask a question? That medicine helped Brooklyn's tummy work more efficiently. Since she doesn't need the painkiller in it now, is there anything you suggest injecting as an enema?"

She gave up pretending not to listen and jumped to her feet. She pulled on his shirt, furiously whispering, "No, Daddy. I don't need that."

"You have a mixture you create for the other Littles? How often should I use it?"

"Daddy," she said, shaking her head.

Caden cradled his phone between his shoulder and jawline to free his hands. With a very stern glance, he steadied her head, preventing her from rattling her brain around. "Alright, experiment to see what helps Brooklyn's tummy most. Start with eight ounces every other Saturday or Sunday afternoon before she naps. Increase to twelve if needed before administering each week. Got it, Zale. Thank you for all your help."

He released her and disconnected from the call. "That was naughty. Don't interrupt Daddy when he's on the phone."

"I don't want more medicine. I'm so much better. My head isn't fuzzy at all," she promised.

"I've noticed how much better you're doing," he said, meeting her gaze directly.

"I should never have told you that my stomach feels better," Brooklyn muttered, vowing silently never to answer questions that might come back to haunt her. Unfortunately, he always distracted her into revealing information. She told him about her stomach problems after several orgasms thanks to that pink interrogation wand vibrator.

"Not telling Daddy the truth would add to your spanking list," Caden warned and pointed at the prominently displayed paper displayed in the kitchen.

Their rules hung on the refrigerator. Brooklyn had four:

1. TALK POSITIVELY *about herself*
2. *tell the truth*
3. *let Daddy know where she is*
4. *no standing on the furniture.*

CADEN HAD THREE:

. . .

1. LISTEN *to his little girl*
   2. *tell the truth*
   3. *help Brooklyn be little.*

BROOKLYN REALLY LIKED the last one most on his list. Trusting Caden came easier now. He pushed her boundaries when she hesitated to act like she craved. She needed his help to get out of her head and simply be.

Wishing to stay positive, Caden had refused to list her punishments, but they had discussed several methods he might use to help her make better decisions. Spanking headed the list. A red number three magnet clung to the freezer to remind him to spank her for lying about the cups and leaving without telling him as well as her other delayed punishments.

"Isn't it important that you feel your best?" Caden asked softly, studying her face.

Brooklyn dropped her gaze down to her pink socks. She didn't want to answer him.

"Doesn't Daddy reward you when you're brave and take your medicine?"

She nodded and wrinkled her nose. He was so logical about everything. Her daddy masterfully explained the positive reasons until she couldn't disagree with him. "But it's embarrassing."

"What do we say in this house?" he asked, tilting her chin up until their gazes met.

"We do whatever is necessary to be happy," she recited.

"Does having Daddy take care of your bottom make your tummy happier?"

She hesitated and peeked back at the list of rules. That no-lying one got her all the time. "Yes, Daddy."

"Good girl. That was very brave of you. Would you like some cuddles on the couch as a reward?"

"Please!" She eliminated the space between them and hugged him tight. "And a sticker."

"I think both can be arranged." He swept Brooklyn up in his arms and carried her on his hip to the refrigerator.

Grabbing a sheet of stickers from his stash on top of the appliance, Caden asked, "Do you want a good girl or a bunny sticker?"

"Good girl!"

"I think that's an excellent choice. Peel off the one you want." When she handed it to him, he placed it on her belly. "There's my good little girl."

"Look, Daddy! My tummy's good too."

"Yes, it is, sweetheart." He rewarded Brooklyn with a steamy kiss before walking to the couch to hold her on his lap.

"Prepare for cuddles," he warned and squeezed her until she squeaked. When she giggled, he eased his hold and ran his hands up and down her back.

Brooklyn relaxed on his hard frame, loving his touch and attention. She could never get enough cuddles.

Twenty minutes later, she battled to keep her eyes open as she yawned widely.

"Nap time, little girl." He stood and carried her to her nursery.

She didn't fuss. Naps were amazing. Caden set her on the soft bedding and eased her clothing off, leaving her only in her diaper. He tucked her under the covers with Fluffikins before kissing her forehead.

"Open for Daddy," he whispered and slid her pacifier between her lips. "Sweet dreams."

She wiggled, getting comfortable, before sighing happily. The soft sheets wrapped around her almost naked body.

Brooklyn smiled softly. Caden enjoyed looking at her. With his help, she was learning to be comfortable in her own skin. The creaking runner of the rocking chair told her that Caden sat by her crib, watching over her as she tumbled into sleep.

***

"Daddy?" Brooklyn called, mumbling around her pacifier.

Silence answered her.

Squirming out from under the covers, she slid on her tummy off the high mattress of her crib. She hugged Fluffikins to her breasts, giggling as his fur tickled her nipples. Daddy would be so happy that she napped so well.

Brooklyn went to see if she'd earned another sticker. The family room and kitchen were empty. She turned in a circle. Where was he? A piece of white paper on the table caught her eye.

Brookie,

They called us in to help with a busted pipe on base. I'll be back as soon as possible. Love you!

Daddy

Wrinkling her nose at the news, Brooklyn headed back to the nursery to play. The slamming of a car door in the driveway caught her attention. Why hadn't her daddy pulled into the garage?

She walked to the front window to peek out with no one seeing her naked. A man with a black hoodie pulled up over his hair walked toward her. He focused completely on his phone. A small breeze ruffled one side of the hood, revealing Brent's face.

Brooklyn ran into the hallway and froze. The months of fear and feeling hunted flooded her mind and body. She struggled to think. What should she do? Fluffikins' fur reminded her she needed clothes. She definitely didn't want to wrangle with Brent like this.

Ripping off her diaper as she dashed for the nursery, Brooklyn threw it into the trash. He couldn't catch her in that. Brooklyn didn't stop to consider how Brent would react to that. Heavy pounding on the door made her jump. Brent would get in, even if he had to break a window. Her heart raced as she grabbed underwear and scrambled into the clothes Caden had put on her that morning.

In full panic mode, Brooklyn struggled to make a plan. If she backed her car out of the driveway, Brent would attack her vehicle. A buzz caught her attention. The phone.

Spotting Daddy on the screen identifying the caller, she grabbed the phone on the rocking chair and whispered into it as the call connected. "Daddy. He's here. Brent. He's trying to get in."

"I'm on my way, little girl. Stay out of sight. If he gets in, grab anything you can use for a weapon. Fight if you have to."

Something thumped on the windows. Thankfully, Caden hadn't opened the blinds that morning. "Brooklyn! Don't make me angrier. Come out and let's go. That military guy isn't coming to save you. They've got a big mess on their hands on base."

She didn't answer. Each word hit her like a stone. She'd experienced Brent's anger before she left. In her gut, she understood this time he wouldn't simply hurt her. He'd kill her.

A murmur of Caden's voice came through the phone line. Outside, Brent paused. Could he hear that? She backed into the hallway and whispered, "Sh! He's listening."

Caden immediately stopped talking. Brooklyn left the line open so he could hear, but stuffed her phone into her bra. She'd try to give him updates about what was happening. Thinking furiously, she searched for a weapon. *The knives in the kitchen!*

Dropping to her knees in case he'd returned to peer into the front windows, Brooklyn crawled behind the furniture to the kitchen. She dared to reach over the counter to grab the block of knives and returned to crouch low on the floor. Brooklyn grabbed a long, thin knife and the big butcher's knife. She placed the block on the floor and eased the oven open. As quietly as possible, she stashed the rest of the set inside. Maybe that would keep him from using the blades on her.

She shuddered at the idea before searching for a hiding spot. The big, open space didn't provide any shelter. If he got inside, Brent would expect her to lock herself in a bathroom or bedroom. He wouldn't expect for her to stay here. Brooklyn turned to the pantry and forced herself forward. She hadn't walked inside that storage room since her accident.

Considering the space inside, Brooklyn saw she had two choices. She could crawl under the bottom shelf and pull a case of water in front of her. If he spotted her there, Brent would loom over her, weakening her efforts to defend herself. A window shattered next in the family room. Brooklyn stood on her tiptoes to set the knives down before grabbing a shelf and climbing. Moving as silently as possible, she clung onto the wood as she shifted the presents that remained on the top shelf.

"Come out, come out, Brooklyn. Why hide? I will find you."

Brooklyn forced herself to move through her terror as he bellowed, using the frightening sound as cover. As she suspected, he'd immediately headed into the hallway. She stretched out on the top shelf and pulled Caden's presents in front of her.

"Fucking bitch! You're always so much trouble," Brent screamed from the back of the house.

He'll be coming soon.

Her trembling shoulders rustled the wrapping paper. Brooklyn struggled to stop the movement. She wanted to talk to her daddy, but in the cramped space she worried she'd knock something off the shelf if she retrieved her phone from under her shirt. Suddenly the volume of Brent's shouts increased, and she guessed he was returning.

"What's that room back there, Brooklyn? Are you pregnant? Dreaming of rocking your bastard baby in that rocking chair?"

Her heart lurched in her chest at the thought he'd invaded her special room. If she survived this, she'd deal with the negativity he'd left in the house.

The knives! She'd forgotten them on the shelf below her. Moving as quickly as she dared, Brooklyn snaked a hand out to reach for them. Her fingers brushed the handles, and she grabbed one.

"Every moment I search for you means more pain for you. I've dreamed of breaking your bones, Brooklyn. Forget London Bridge is falling down, I'm going to watch Brooklyn Bridge fall down—even if I have to shatter your shins to bring you down."

Brooklyn grabbed for the second knife, slicing her finger on the blade. She bit her lip to stop herself from crying out and trailed along the metal to the wooden handle. *Please get here, Daddy. Please!*

Light appeared along the edges of the pantry door as he pushed it open. Peeking between the packages in front of her face, Brooklyn could see him scan the room. His first move? Brent kicked the case of water on the floor.

Biting her lip, Brooklyn celebrated her decision not to hide there. Brent searched the bottom shelves, tossing boxes and small appliances like the toaster as she held her breath. His gaze rose higher, and he scanned the storage area below her. He was going to find her.

"Presents? Did your soldier buy you something special, Brooklyn? You've fooled him just like you pulled the wool over my eyes."

Time seemed to freeze as he reached up for the package in front of her. When his fingers wrapped around the box in front of her face, Brooklyn thrust the sharp blade forward.

His scream turned her blood to ice. Brent recoiled, falling against the open door with a loud bang. Brooklyn struggled to think quickly. What should she do?

Brent lunged forward. The silence now seemed deadly without his threats. A thick arm stopped Brent in his tracks, and she recognized Caden's buzz cut as he yanked Brent into the kitchen. She could hear Brent's yells and thuds.

"Go get your girl. We've got this." That wasn't her daddy. Was the entire team in the house? She hadn't heard any of them.

Caden appeared in the doorway. He reached out immediately to sweep her off the shelf. His urgent motion swept the presents off the shelf without a second thought. Her daddy hugged her hard to his chest as he carried her out of the house into the driveway as sirens filled the air.

CHAPTER 20

*B*rooklyn insisted on attending his trial. The evidence presented to the judge was so overwhelming on the first morning that his court-appointed lawyer asked for a recess to talk to Brent before they resumed in the afternoon. When the judge reconvened court after lunch, Brooklyn gasped as Brent's lawyer announced a plea deal.

Standing with slumped shoulders, Brent didn't turn to glare at her. His gaze remained fixed on the table in front of him. She listened to him plead guilty to multiple charges of robbery and assault. Stalking her hadn't landed him in jail; his illegal actions during the long months while he searched for her had put him away for years.

"Is it over, Daddy?" Brooklyn whispered as they dragged Brent from the courtroom.

"It's over, sweetheart. He won't ever bother you again," Caden reassured her. "Max had a talk with him during the break. Brent understands he'll be safer in jail than walking around."

It wasn't like the other promises she'd heard from the police and lawyers. Caden's words rang with truth.

"Max talked to him?" she repeated in astonishment.

"Yes. I couldn't trust myself to be that close to him. Let's go home, little girl. Max and the guys are waiting for us there."

She stared at the door where Brent had disappeared. *Could it really be over?* Her daddy placed a hand on her lower back and guided her toward the door. Brooklyn remained silent until they exited into the fresh air.

The breeze helped her understand that this was actually happening. Brooklyn had met three times already with a counselor who worked near the base. With the therapist's help, she was working through the frightening memories that Brent had subjected her to before and after she'd left. Feeling lighter than she had in years, Brooklyn looked up at her daddy and asked, "Is this what freedom is like?"

"I can't wait to show you how amazing your life is going to be now, Brookie. Ready to go let the team celebrate with you?"

"Let's go, Daddy."

"Brooklyn?"

She turned to see Brent's mother, Suzanne standing a couple of feet away. Brooklyn wrapped her hands around Caden's arm, clinging to him for support.

"I didn't mean to scare you," the woman said quickly, not getting any closer. "We wanted you to know that we tried to get him to stop coming after you when several months passed. He wouldn't listen to us. Hopefully, he'll get some help in jail."

"As long as he's far from me, I don't care what happens to him," Brooklyn said bluntly. A small part of her noted that his family hadn't helped him pursue her after the initial months. That made her feel better—slightly better.

"Our family wishes you well, Brooklyn. I'm glad you found a man who treats you right," Suzanne told her and left with a nod to rejoin her husband and daughter.

"Barbecue time, little girl. Let's get on the road. Koa has a bad reputation for torching food. We don't want him to cook without supervision," Caden told her.

"Wait. Giana's a firefighter."

"You'll have to ask her how they met," Caden suggested, steering her off the sidewalk to the parking lot.

"Okay. I'm going to ask Aspen and Pippa, too."

"Good idea," Caden said, lifting her up into his truck.

"I'm really glad I found you," Brooklyn whispered as her daddy fastened her seatbelt.

"Me, too, little girl. I can't imagine my world without you." He kissed her softly and stepped back to close her door.

Caden drove carefully through the traffic back to the house Brooklyn now considered home. As the truck turned onto their street, Brooklyn leaned forward to peer through the window. Trucks and SUVs lined the road.

"Is Max carrying a ladder?" she asked, spotting the large man from several houses away. "He's got paint splattered on his shirt."

"Max has been busy, little girl."

"Really? What's he been doing?"

"I think this is something you need to see rather than me telling you," Caden suggested as he pulled into the driveway next to Max's huge SUV.

It took forever for her daddy to circle around the hood to let her out. Brooklyn decided not to wait. She flung open the door and jumped out. A cry burst from her lips as Brooklyn caught her heel in her skirt and tumbled into the grass.

"Are you okay, Brooklyn Marie?" Caden said, running his hands over her.

"I'm fine. Just clumsy," Brooklyn said as her face heated with embarrassment.

"You've scraped up your knee. Let's go clean and bandage that," Caden said, scooping her up in his arms.

"But Max did something inside. I want to see," she whined.

"Knee, spanking, surprise."

"Spanking?" Brooklyn said in surprise as he entered their house.

"We heard what happened," Giana said excitedly.

They shouted their congratulations as Caden continued walking through the family room toward their bedroom.

"Thanks for coming, everyone. Carry on without us. I have a little girl to talk to privately. We'll be back in a few."

Caden carried her into their bedroom and closed the door before entering the bathroom. He set her on the vanity and braced a hand on each side of her. "Who opens the truck door, little girl?"

"Me when I'm alone," she sassed.

"Are you alone, Brooklyn Marie?"

"No. But you were going so slowly. I wanted to see what Max had done."

"And you hurt yourself because you were going too fast. Which was wiser?" he asked, pinning her in place with a stern look.

She pouted for several long seconds before finally answering, "I guess slower."

"I agree. Now, what hurts other than your knee?"

"I banged my elbow, too," she admitted, guessing that Caden would strip her naked to check for himself if she didn't tell the truth.

Caden nodded and kissed her forehead. "Does your head hurt?"

"No. I'm okay," she reassured him. Zale had cleared her of any restrictions because of her concussion. She hadn't had any headaches for several weeks.

"Good." Caden immediately got to work, cleaning and bandaging her scrape. He checked her elbow and promised to get the frozen peas out to treat her. Then he lifted her from the vanity and stripped off her panties.

"Daddy, no! People are here. You can't spank me," Brooklyn protested.

Caden didn't answer. He took a seat on the bed and draped Brooklyn over his hard thighs. Flipping her dress up, he smacked her bottom hard. "You are not to open the door, little girl."

Each swat from his powerful hands left a stinging spot on her skin. Brooklyn flailed her legs, trying to avoid the punishment, but Caden held her pinned firmly in place.

She tried to stay quiet as the heat and pain built. Each stroke of his hand erased a bit of the worry that had built inside her from the stress of Brent's court appearance. She couldn't think of anything but the small space that surrounded them. Finally, sobs burst through her lips as she slumped over his lap. Her punishment continued until she whispered, "I'm sorry, Daddy."

At those magic words, Caden's touch switched from punishing to soothing. His hand rubbed over her bottom as he praised her. "There's my good little girl. I knew she was in there."

Caden lifted her back to his arms and rocked her gently on his lap. "This has been a tough week for you. I think you needed Daddy's attention. Do you feel better?" he asked.

She nodded against his chest. "So much better."

After clearing her list of delayed spankings and earning new ones, Brooklyn had learned that she hated and loved spankings. The good-girl spankings were wonderful and always preceded a flurry of reward orgasms. The others? Well, she hated to admit they created another kind of release she needed just as bad. Somehow, her daddy could read her as easily as he entertained her with storybooks.

After several breaths, Brooklyn pushed away from his chest, hissing as her weight settled fully on her bottom. "They all know I got a spanking, don't they?"

"Yes." Her daddy followed his rules completely and never lied to her.

"Like Aspen who got a spanking at the last gathering," Brooklyn suggested, remembering the sound of her friend's cries from her nursery. All the Littles had welcomed her back with hugs when Aspen had returned. No one commented on her blotchy face at all.

"Let's go erase these tears and greet our company properly," Caden told her.

With her face clean of the makeup she'd worn to court, Brooklyn clung to her daddy's hand as she followed him to the kitchen. Aspen, Giana, and Pippa crowded around her in a flurry of greetings. Brooklyn turned from the last embrace to meet Max's kind gaze.

"I think your daddy has a surprise for you," the large man suggested.

"Let's go check out your nursery," Caden said, sweeping a hand toward the hallway.

Brooklyn forced herself to walk to the closed door. Turning the knob, she peeked into the room and gasped. She pushed the door open and bounced inside, turning to look at the walls.

Ever since Brent had been inside her nursery, it hadn't felt the same. Like his presence had somehow left a shadow over the beautiful room. No darkness could exist in this area ever again. The walls were a bright sunny yellow with flowers, cute animals, and smiling insects. It was like being in the middle of a gorgeous meadow.

She walked forward to touch one grinning ladybug. Caden caught her hand. "It's wet, little girl. You don't want to smudge Max's work."

Whirling to stare at the large man now standing in the room with the others, Brooklyn asked, "You painted all of this?" Her first impression of the burly soldier aligned better with cutting firewood with an axe than holding a paintbrush.

"I did. I almost skipped joining the military to go paint pictures in Paris," Max told her with a wink.

"Thank you so much." Brooklyn ran forward to throw her arms around his waist. The impact with his hard body felt like running into a wall. "Oof!"

"Careful there, Brooklyn. You don't have to thank me. I was glad to paint you an army of cute friends to guard you," Max told her.

Brooklyn turned to scan the room one more time. He was right. She could never be scared in this room with all these creatures to back her up.

"I love this so much," she whispered.

"You're going to have to name them," Pippa suggested.

"Want to help me?" Brooklyn asked, grinning at her friends.

As the Littles debated different names, Brooklyn overheard the men talking behind them.

"I decided to take an art class at the local community college," Max told the guys.

"Are you going to sit around and paint fruit?" Koa asked.

"No, it's a human figure drawing class. We'll have models," Max explained.

"Clothed?" Hank asked.

"Sometimes," Max answered.

"Maybe I should take this art class with you," Hank said.

"You'll have to qualify by showing them your portfolio," Max told him.

"I've seen you sketch wiring plans for explosives," Jerico said. "They'll bump you back to art history."

"Probably. Looks like you'll have to excel on your own, Max," Hank told him. "Let's go eat. All this talk about models makes me hungry."

"Alright, Littles. Let's go raid the food," Caden suggested, holding a hand out for Brooklyn's.

She skipped to his side. "Let's go, Daddy! I'm starving." As they walked, she whispered, "Can I sit on a cushion?"

"No way, little girl. Sitting on your hot bottom might remind you to make better decisions."

Brooklyn pouted for the rest of the way to the kitchen. When he settled her at the kitchen table with a plate of her favorite foods and chocolate milk, she couldn't help but smile at him. He showed her each day how much he loved her.

Her gaze fell on the pile of presents Caden had moved to a low shelf by the table. She'd struggled to walk back into the pantry after that last encounter with Brent. While they worked on erasing the bad memories in the small room, Caden had stored the gifts where she could easily reach them. She'd opened one more the last time during his last, thankfully quick, deployment. Even her sore bottom reminded her how her dreams had come true.

"Thank you, Daddy. I'm the luckiest little girl in the world."

"And I'm the luckiest daddy." He kissed her lightly before scooting her chair up to the table. "Eat. I want to see that plate empty."

"Your daddy takes good care of you, Brooklyn," Pippa told her, waving a fork laden with macaroni and cheese.

"He does. He makes everything better," Brooklyn said.

"That's what daddies are for. Who do you think will find their little girl next?" Aspen asked. "My vote's on Hank."

"No, it has to be Max," Brooklyn said. "I think he'll be a great daddy."

The End

AFTERWORD

Stormy Night Publications would like to thank you for your interest in our books.

If you liked this book (or even if you didn't), we would really appreciate you leaving a review on the site where you purchased it. Reviews provide useful feedback for us and our authors, and this feedback (both positive comments and constructive criticism) allows us to work even harder to make sure we provide the content our customers want to read.

If you would like to check out more books from Stormy Night Publications, if you want to learn more about our company, or if you would like to join our mailing list, please visit our website at:

http://www.stormynightpublications.com

BOOKS OF THE SOLDIER DADDIES SERIES

The Medic's Little Girl

When stern, handsome army medic Doniphan Williams asks her out, it isn't long before twenty-three-year-old waitress River Reynolds blushingly admits her need for a firm-handed daddy. But daddies expect to be obeyed, and when River doesn't keep in touch as instructed while Doniphan is away on a mission she quickly ends up over his knee for a sound spanking on her bare bottom.

As she is held in Doniphan's arms after her punishment, River feels more safe and loved than she ever has before, and when he claims her properly it is more pleasurable than she could have ever imagined. Soon she is quivering with need as he takes her temperature and gives her a thorough, intimate examination, but will she be a good girl for daddy even when he puts her in diapers?

Tex's Little Girl

When a big, strong, handsome soldier tells off a customer who was treating her poorly, pastry chef Rosie Perez soon finds herself baking cookies for her rescuer… and calling him daddy.

Tex is the kind of daddy who will cuddle her when she's upset. He's also the kind who will take his little girl over his knee and spank her bare bottom very soundly when she's been naughty, then bathe her and put her to bed in her nursery to remind her that she's not a big girl anymore.

Though Rosie blushes crimson as Tex diapers her for the first time, when he takes her in his arms and claims her properly it is the most pleasure she has ever experienced. But when she has to visit the doctor will she be a good girl for daddy or will her bottom be bright red for her exam?

Jax's Little Girl

Jax Wescott isn't the kind of man who ignores a woman in need of assistance, and when he witnesses Ember Stevens having a panic attack in a park he gently helps her through it. But it quickly becomes clear that Ember is in need of quite a bit more than just a hug and a pep talk.

She needs a daddy. A daddy who will not just take care of her, but take charge of her as well.

A daddy like Jax.

Though she sobs as she is spanked very soundly on her bare bottom for being reckless with her safety and blushes crimson when she is put to bed in a nursery, being held in Jax's arms and claimed properly is better than she could have ever dreamed. But will she behave herself when the time comes for daddy to take her to the doctor for a very thorough, embarrassing exam?

Sam's Little Girl

As she enjoys her cotton candy at the state fair the last thing twenty-two-year-old Hope Anderson expects is to end up riding the Ferris wheel with a handsome special ops soldier who calls her little girl, but Sam Memphis knows a woman in need of a daddy when he sees one.

Hope soon learns the hard way that Sam meant what he said about naughty girls getting a sound spanking, and it isn't long before she's being put in a diaper with her bottom still bright red. She delights in every moment of her daddy's intimate attention even when it leaves her blushing, but will a visit to the doctor for a very thorough exam prove more embarrassing than she can bear?

The Captain's Little Girl

Though Captain Mark Cunningham has wanted beautiful waitress Cricket Wilson to be his little girl for years, he's old enough to be her father and he's always told himself he isn't right for her. But when the battle-hardened special forces officer barely makes it home alive from a dangerous assignment, he decides it is time to do what he should have done ages ago and claim her as his.

Cricket is delighted when the handsome soldier she's dreamed about for so long finally takes her in his arms, and no matter how bright red she blushes she has never felt safer and more loved than when he bathes her, puts her in diapers, and even brings her to the medic for a very intimate exam. But when a mission puts her new daddy behind enemy lines will she lose him forever?

Jerico's Little Girl

Twenty-five-year-old Aspen Randolph has always dreamed of a big, strong daddy who would take her in hand and make sure she feels safe and loved, and when special forces officer Jerico Adams steps in to rescue her from a threatening situation her dream suddenly becomes reality.

But Jerico doesn't just plan to make Aspen's troubles his business. He plans to make her his.

Sometimes that will mean spanking her when she's naughty, then bathing her and putting her down for a nap with her bottom still stinging. Other times it will mean bringing her to the doctor for a thorough examination, or even putting her in diapers despite how bright red she blushes.

Most of all, though, it means she can trust daddy to take care of her no matter what.

Zale's Little Girl

After gorgeous army medic Zale Reynolds saves Pippa Twinner from a kidnapper, he doesn't just bring her home with him and make it his business to take care of her. He makes her call him daddy too.

Though she blushes crimson as her ruggedly handsome rescuer bathes her, puts her to bed, and takes her temperature the old-fashioned way, Pippa cherishes his loving attention, and when he takes her over his knee and spanks her bare bottom, she doesn't just promise to be a very good girl for her new daddy.

She comes really hard for him too.

Koa's Little Girl

Giana felt brave as she left the note with that simple question at the base for special forces officer Koa Lokela, but the moment he gave her his answer she was soaking wet and blushing crimson.

Now he's undressing her and carrying her to his bed to claim her as his not just in her naughtiest fantasies but for real.

And soon he'll be spanking her bare bottom when she's been a bad girl, bathing her and tucking her in with a kiss after a hard day, and sometimes even putting her in diapers, taking her temperature, or bringing her to the squad medic for a thorough examination while he watches.

Because his answer was yes.

MORE STORMY NIGHT BOOKS BY PEPPER NORTH

A Polar Hope (included in *Marked Brides: Six Alpha Shifter Romances*)

After losing her job on Earth, Marisol signs up for a cultural exchange program with Terra Arcus, but upon her arrival she is stripped and put up for auction. When the northern clan chief recognizes her as his own, he claims her and escorts her back to his lands. While their future children are the hope for the clan's survival, she captures her stern mate's heart as well. He will ease her adaptation to her new life with a firm hand and a loving embrace.

A Polar Second Chance (included in *Claimed Brides: Seven Alpha Shifter Romances*)

Ruth would have never expected to experience a connection with the seer of Clan Thorben, but merely touching the handsome polar bear shifter's hand leaves her feeling warm in a way she never has before. But he doesn't plan for her to be just his mate. She will be his little girl also, to be loved, cherished, and spanked very soundly on her bare bottom when she's been naughty.

PEPPER NORTH LINKS

You can keep up with Pepper North via her website, her Twitter account, her Facebook page, her Amazon page, and her Goodreads profile, using the following links:

https://4peppernorth.club/
https://twitter.com/4peppernorth
https://www.facebook.com/PepperNorthauthor
https://www.amazon.com/stores/Pepper-North/author/B072MWDRD4
https://www.goodreads.com/author/show/16941120.Pepper_North

Printed in Dunstable, United Kingdom